Dragonfire Trail

You could call them 'blood brothers': they had shed plenty of their own blood during the savage battles of the War. And it had mingled more than once.

Afterwards, they rode together, getting into and out of scrapes, watching each other's back, sidekicks and friends. Then that old enemy and infamous disrupter struck gold. Lots of it. Already tainted with blood.

The only way it could be settled was over blazing guns.

Dragonfire Trail

Hank J. Kirby

A Black Horse Western

ROBERT HALE · LONDON

ISBN 978-0-7090-8789-2

Robert Hale Limited
Clerkenwell House
Clerkenwell Green
London EC1R 0HT

www.halebooks.com

Typeset by
Derek Doyle & Associates, Shaw Heath
Printed and bound in Great Britain by
CPI Antony Rowe, Chippenham and Eastbourne

PROLOGUE

SORT OF GUILTY

The stagecoach hold-up attempt went wrong right from the start. Caine even claimed it wasn't any such thing.

But the shotgun guard and the driver dragged him into town, trussed like a Thanksgiving turkey, and Caine told the sheriff his name was 'Frank Keller'.

'Trail man, Sheriff,' he added. He looked like a regular cowboy, a 'trail hand' as he claimed, but there was a certain hardness about the wide mouth, and the eyes flashed in a cold warning when Canning, the big rough deputy, prodded him in the back, sending him staggering into the law office.

'Trail hand – or outlaw?' suggested Sheriff Larson, a heavy, lazy-looking man who ran a mostly law-abiding town and county. He was irritated at having his easy routine upset by the likes of this would-be stage robber.

'Aw, look, you fellers've got it all wrong. Tell you what really happened. . . .'

He jerked and straightened, grimacing, as Canning rammed a rigid knuckle into his kidney region. 'We know what happened. The driver and guard told us – we don't need no lies from you.'

That was when the sheriff saw the deadly bleakness in Caine's eyes as they briefly raked the deputy.

'My horse stepped in a gopher hole, Sheriff. Threw me, but he couldn't have been hurt much 'cause the damn jughead ran off, left me afoot on the edge of the badlands.'

'Better places to be left afoot,' the sheriff observed, but Canning merely twitched his big nostrils, waiting for another chance to prod Caine.

'Hell, yeah!' Caine agreed, hoping to get the sheriff onside. 'I started walking, seen a dust cloud coming and figured it was the stage to Broken Bend. Ran towards it, waving like my arm was about to fly off – but the driver didn't see me. So, I drew my six-gun, aiming to fire off a couple shots to get his attention.'

The deputy spluttered disbelievingly.

'Not the way the shotgun guard saw it, son. He claims you started to run towards the stage, waving that Colt like you was decidin' who to shoot, him or the driver.'

'Hell, no! See, that's what I mean, Sheriff. I guess it could've looked that way, but I swear I—'

'Aw, shut up!' Canning growled and knuckled Caine's spine brutally. 'We ain't interested in fairy stories.'

Straightening painfully, Caine quickly stepped forward, hands still cuffed behind his back, and snapped his head into Canning's arrogant face. His forehead crunched the big man's nose. Blood spurted and the deputy staggered back, one leg buckling. His eyes filled with tears of pain and his jaw dripped blood. Then he was spluttering curses as he reached for his six-gun.

'Leave it, Nick!' growled Sheriff Larson, and had to repeat the order twice before Canning let his gun drop back into the holster. He fumbled up a red-checked kerchief and held it to his bleeding nose, eyes blazing above the cloth.

He didn't say anything – it was all in the look; Caine would pay for that.

'You sit down, Keller,' the sheriff snapped and Canning eagerly grabbed Caine's wide shoulders and slammed him down into a straight-back chair so hard it almost overturned. 'What really happened, Mr Keller, was that you tried to *hold up* the stage, *not flag it down.*'

Caine shook his head. 'No, no, Sheriff. I know that's how it must've seemed. I tripped on a rock, see, that's why it looked like I was *running* at 'em. I stumbled forward, sort of and—'

'You were lucky the guard was a new man, not trigger-happy, and he wasn't sure whether to shoot or not. That's all that saved you from a charge of buckshot.'

Caine nodded. 'Glad I had some luck!'

'Not much,' growled the deputy with a tight grin as he lowered the blood-sodden kerchief. 'You're lookin' at about five years on the rockpile – I'm glad to say.'

Caine's jaw dropped and he flicked his gaze to Larson. 'That – that gospel, Sheriff?'

The lawman nodded slowly. 'At least. No one's gonna believe that crazy story you're tryin' to put over on us, son. . . . You realize you'll be frontin'-up to Judge Cobb here?'

Caine licked his lips, looked from one man to the other, seemed to make a decision. 'Hell – he sends everyone to the big pen!'

'No jury here, son,' he was told with a certain satisfaction. 'Judge Cobb pre-sides and de-cides.' The sheriff flicked his gaze to Canning and smiled slightly. 'And I'm here to tell you, he don't make many "not guilty" decisions.'

Despite his pain, Canning guffawed, watching Caine wilt at this information. 'I can't recollect *any*.'

'Well, hell, I didn't know I was in *his* county. . . .' Caine dragged down a deep breath and nodded slightly; he had made a decision. 'All right. I paid off from a trail herd and I had . . . quite a few drinks before I rode out of town.'

Canning chuckled. 'They gonna have to last you a long, long time, feller.'

The sheriff signed to the deputy to let Caine speak.

'Well – my horse did run off. That's gospel. So's trying to flag down the stage, but. . . . On the spur of the moment, when I seen the shotgun guard hadn't picked up his Greener, guess I had a crazy thought or two, figurin' if there was a shotgun guard, there must be a strongbox on board, you know? And this was a mighty lonely place at the edge of the badlands. I was tempted, but I never tried to hold 'em up. Then I tripped on a rock and the guard got the drop on me. I didn't *do* anything, never hurt no one!'

'We'll see what Judge Cobb has to say about that. Put him in the cells, Nick. And I don't want to hear he fell down them stone steps on the way and hurt himself. OK?'

Tight-lipped, Canning nodded reluctantly.

At his 'trial', still using the name of Frank Keller, Caine tried to explain it to Judge Cobb, a prune-mouthed bitter-looking man with a shock of grey hair, some pink scalp showing through. The judge also suffered with a stomach ulcer and it was acting up like a mule with colic that day. He paused to snatch a handful of peppermints from a small crumpled paper bag and chewed them, waving a hand for the accused to be seated; Caine had stood up in his eagerness to tell his version of what had happened.

It was just the opportunity Canning was waiting for.

He stepped up behind Caine and kicked his legs hard. They folded and Caine staggered, missed the chair, floundered on the floor. The packed courtroom laughed – but the crowd gasped a moment later when Caine surged up and, hands still manacled, kicked the deputy between the legs. Canning collapsed, moaning.

There was a lot of shouting and running and Caine was manhandled mighty roughly by the court attendants. He was bleeding from nose and mouth and a cut above his left eye when they eventually rammed him into his chair, hard enough to jar his spine. Canning was still huddled in a corner, holding his nether regions, and looking mighty sick.

Judge Cobb glared at Caine. He grimaced as bile surged up into his gullet.

'Mister, you are one violent man, ain't you? I heard about you spreading Deputy Canning's nose all over his face – and now this. Well, you haven't done your case a power of good, you realize that?'

'Judge, he's been prodding and poking and kicking my shins ever since they brought me in.'

'You don't inspire gentle treatment, Mr Keller. You have the look of a mighty hard man on a short fuse.'

'I've led a hard life, Judge. But don't keep me in suspense any longer. Get it over with – quicker I start serving my sentence, sooner it'll be finished.'

Judge Cobb burped and smiled thinly. 'Well, men in your position aren't usually so eager to know their fate – but I'll oblige you, Mr Keller. How does seven years in the territorial penitentiary sound to you?' The judge leaned forward, smiling tightly, enjoying delivering the harsh sentence. 'That's hard time, of course.'

There was a sharp indrawing of breath from the crowd. Then they gawked as Caine suddenly smiled widely and nodded to the bench.

'Thank you kindly, Judge – *muchas gracias*. I'll be thinking of you – every minute of those seven years.'

Cobb's thin lips rippled into a bitter, sour smile.

'Do I detect a threat in there, Mr Keller? We could try for ten, if you're so inclined. . . ?'

'Aw, I think seven'll be long enough, Judge. I wouldn't want to play on your – generosity.'

Judge Cobb frowned. 'Tell me – why the hell do I get the feeling that you're enjoying this, Keller?'

Caine shrugged. 'Mostly because I am, I guess.'

Cobb gave an involuntary rumbling burp and shook his head slowly, reaching for his bag of peppermints as they led Caine away.

Goddamnit! The man was – whistling!

CHAPTER 1

HELL HOLE

One thing about the rockpile: it got you out into the open, away from the stench and scum, damp and discomfort of the cellblocks. But it did have its drawbacks, mostly too many guards looking to bust a head or two.

There was a bigger population in here than Caine had seen in some towns. It was *crowded* no matter where you went within the thick greystone walls of the buildings; men rubbed shoulders whenever they moved, and the guards seemed to take delight in forcing them all together, cramming extra prisoners into confined spaces, then watching from the high observation galleries as tempers flared and accusations of groping and assault were made. There wasn't much room for brawling but somehow there was always blood spilled and hide bruised or bones broken. Home-made knives – laboriously fashioned from broken files, even

12

long nails or rusted pieces of sheet iron, by rubbing on the stone floors or walls until they took on some sort of edge and point – were produced. And used.

Many a time a packed crowd dispersed on orders from the guards and there, left on the ground, would be the writhing body of a wounded man, or even a corpse – and everyone looked completely innocent as they shuffled away, as surprised as the guards when the victims were revealed.

Many grudges were settled during the 'cattle calls' as the guards named these crowded and obligatory assemblies.

So far, Caine had had no more than a fist in the gut or someone groping to twist his balls; each time he had managed to poke a bony elbow into the eye of the man who tried. Once, in the yard, hidden by a pile of newly blasted rocks, another inmate with some fancied grudge tried to brain him with a crowbar. He heard it whistling as it descended and long-time, well-honed instinct took him away from the fall of the bar. It clanged and clattered on the broken granite and the man who had swung it yelled and jumped, dropping the tool as it jarred all the way up his arms into his shoulders and neck.

There were two or three of his cronies there, too, but they weren't fast enough to stop Caine from swinging his fourteen-pound sledge on to the foot of the man who had tried to kill him. There were plenty of screams and the guards came a-running, big boots thudding rapidly over the broken ground as they charged in, short carbines and shotguns cocked.

13

By the time they reached the man with the crushed foot, one of the other inmates was rolling a big rock aside, gasping as he told the nearest guard,

'Rolled down – right on to his – foot.'

The unwritten law of the pen was that inmates settled their own troubles – they wanted no help from guards.

The guard looked at the mangled flesh and protruding bones and the foot's grey-faced owner, then swung the butt of his carbine into the belly of the man who had rolled the rock aside. The prisoner gagged and dropped to his knees, forehead touching the ground as he hugged himself. The guard swung a heavy boot into the man's raised backside, driving his face into the ground.

'You call me "sir", you lousy trash!'

'I – I'm sorry – sir. Rock – heavy – lost me – breath.'

'You'll lose your teeth next time,' the guard growled. 'Get this man over to the infirmary.' He raked his hostile gaze around at the prisoners gawking in their ragged clothes. 'Anyone tell you to take a rest. . . ?'

The men went back to work immediately, hammers swinging, crowbars prising, rolling rocks – all under the edgy gazes of the armed guards . . . ever watchful for some transgression, big or small, they could act upon.

'That damn O'Rourke,' whispered the shaggy man helping Caine move a rock. 'He knows it weren't no rock busted Carmody's foot. You best rub dirt on your hammerhead and get rid of the blood.'

'Already done.'

'Keller – you say you never been in a big pen before – but – well, you're plenty savvy.'

14

Caine said nothing as they lifted the rock and threw it down to a pile on the level below.

'What'd that feller do – apart from tryin' to brain you with the crowbar?'

'Asked too many questions.'

The man stepped back at Caine's tone, forced a nervous smile. 'I'm Mendez – Manny to my friends.'

'You'll get your "friends" into a heap of trouble you keep talking on the job,' Caine told him, barely moving his lips. He straightened and walked away, hefting his hammer. Sweat and grime rippled on his biceps showing beneath the ragged, torn-off sleeves of the filthy shirt. His fringing brown beard was also clogged with dirt. Prisoners were hosed down only once a week.

Caine, alias Frank Keller, had tried his luck at the 'trial', by hoping to make the judge believe he wanted to be sentenced to the penitentiary. In which case he thought that Cobb might have been cantankerous enough to decide to send him somewhere else – just an attempt to hassle Ray after what he had pulled – but it had backfired. And here he was. . . .

The place was a hell-hole.

The inmates were treated like sub-humans; the food was little better than the swill fed to pigs; they slept in dormitories on long plank benches with worn, thin blankets riddled with vermin. The guards were brutal and had a free hand; it was rumoured that the warden's experience was gained in Andersonville during the War.

If a man was lucky enough to serve out his sentence without being crippled, it was certain-sure he would

15

bust a gut to avoid ever coming back. That was how they justified the place's existence: *we never see repeat offenders*, was the motto. That and *No one ever escapes Bear Creek Pen*. . . .

What the hell am I doing here. . . ?

Caine asked himself that question for maybe the hundredth time since his arrival.

A couple of weeks and it was already too damn long; he couldn't help but wonder if the deal was going to be worth it. He was here now so he might as well follow through.

Damn Ray Porteus! He hadn't given him a true picture of this corner of hell. . . .

'Lying by omission,' he gritted, half-aloud, and one of the men sitting on the hard form next to him, called Lomas, snapped his head up. 'You say what. . . ?'

Caine looked at him bleakly. The man was edgy, belligerent – this could be just what he wanted.

'I said – stop slurping your damn grub! I know it's no better'n pig-swill, and it makes me want to throw up just to look at it. But you make me sick, listenin' to your gurgles and spittin' and chompin'. Hogs wouldn't even let you near the trough, you're so damn disgusting!'

That was it. He got no further before Lomas jumped up, swinging his half-full wooden bowl, the food spraying out in a wide arc. It splashed several other men at the long table as a guard came charging up – just in time to get dollops of slop down his trousers.

He roared and his wooden billy lashed out. Caine ducked and Lomas instinctively lifted an arm protectively. The bone crunched under the club and he shouted, bared his teeth and, without thought, grabbed the guard by the throat. The man's arms flailed and Caine snatched the billy from him, slammed it across the guard's head.

Lomas looked startled as he released the unconscious man, letting him fall across the form. He stared at the billy in Caine's hand, then backed off; he wanted no part of this!

Other guards were rushing in, thrusting inmates aside, one even running down the centre of the table over the food bowls and any hands that didn't get out of the way of his thudding boots soon enough. He launched himself at Caine, who instinctively struck out with the billy. The man fell unconscious and Caine backed against the wall, menacing with the club.

The guards stopped, forming a small threatening arc. Then one of them drew his revolver, cocked the hammer.

Caine shrugged and let the billy fall, lifting his hands. He gave a quick, on-off smile.

'Don't tell me I'm in trouble. . . .'

They closed in swiftly, clubs rising and falling, boots and fists swinging, and, except for the pain, that was all he remembered for a long time.

After moaning and groaning for an unknown length of time, spitting congealed blood from a cut mouth, blowing more from clogged nostrils, he finally figured out where he was.

It was pitch dark and airless. Only one narrow window, very high up, no sounds. His groping hands, as he crawled around the small space – about five feet by four, he estimated – told him there was no bunk, no slop bucket, not even a blanket. Just the cold flagstone floor.

He sat back in a corner, knees drawn up to his bruised chest. Then he laughed – more a cackle than a laugh – the sound eerie in the cold, dark silence.

He had made it to solitary, the Devil's Hole, the inmates called it – to be avoided at all cost.

But he was here, now, in his own stinking, dark little corner of the hell-hole. . . . *At last!*

CHAPTER 2

GETTING THERE

They first met during the War, Joshua Caine and Ray Porteus, separated from their companies, looking for any kind of sanctuary – anything to get away from all the blood and suffering to no end. And the unstoppable Yankees. . . .

It was early 1865 and the Confederacy's long slide into oblivion was well advanced: at this stage it was gathering speed and hurtling towards the inevitable. Chaos reigned. Troops decided they had had enough and simply walked away from battle; if an over-zealous officer was fool enough to try and stop them he was shot, or run through with the long bayonet. Supply columns were not only short, but mostly non-existent. No one could be sure where the troops were, or even what they were doing; this regiment should be *here* but, *no*, it had simply disappeared, no one knew where. A train should arrive at *this* depot in three days. *Two weeks*

19

later beleaguered men were still waiting, starving, dying, without medical supplies, while the mangled tracks where the derailed train had been blown up were slowly rusting in days of endless, heavy, freezing rain.

Officers who had commanded companies in blistering battles now found themselves in charge of only three or four ragged, dull-eyed men nursing rifles without bullets. Others staggered their way south, searching for homes that no longer existed. Lawlessness and insubordination were rife. Murder, rape, pillage. . . . The victims were not only helpless civilians, some in worse shape than the deserting soldiers, but the army itself became a prime target for such men.

They had had enough; they were called 'Johnny Rebs', so they aimed to live up to that name, and to hell with it.

Someone had to pay for the years of hell and horror – and it wasn't going to be them. The Cause had been lost for over a year, so let what remained of the South and its few assets foot the bill.

A food wagon was a bonanza, straining bellies that hadn't known fullness for years. But an arms wagon was as good as currency: guns commanded high prices. The officers in charge of any isolated supply wagons were shot out of hand if they didn't co-operate and approve the plundering. Sometimes those wagons contained the stuff of dreams: weapons by the hundreds that could be sold in Mexico for a small fortune; and, just occasionally, chests of money destined for a pay bill that would now never be honoured. And, sometimes, though rarely, and the cause for extreme celebration – there was gold.

Coins – bars – jewellery, donated in desperation by frightened but still fanatical men and women who saw nothing but defeat, yet gave their last valuables to help keep the South fighting on for one more week – another day – one more hour. . . .

Caine and Porteus, enlisting at fifteen years of age, had fought for the South as men for over three years. Now, both were still boys, barely eighteen, with the South's inevitable surrender only weeks away. They found themselves forcibly recruited as members of an escort troop taking a rare wagonload of gold to a fanatic general who had sworn on his Bible he would die rather than surrender.

He believed he spoke for every man under his command, remnants of the ragtag army of the South; believed they would follow him willingly to Hell or Glory. Still, he gave them no choice in the end: the General made it an order. 'We die for Southern honour!'

'Not me,' said young Ray Porteus, shivering in his torn poncho as cold rain worked through to his ragged clothing while the general's words faded in the roar of yet another heavy downpour. 'I've given enough already: three years of my life! They ain't gettin' what's left!'

His words brought Josh Caine's dark head snapping around, shivering, with only an old cornsack across his shoulders as protection against the elements.

'Hush, you blamed fool!' he hissed. 'They'll shoot

you on the spot if they hear!'

'Uh-uh. I'm cuttin' outta here, Josh. This is a suicide deal. That general's plumb loco. Just look at his eyes! Christ, I'll be seein' them crazy, red-lined eyeballs startin' out of his head every damn night for the rest of my life, I reckon!'

'Judas, will you be *quiet*! You'll get us both killed!'

'No I won't. 'Cause we ain't gonna be around when General In-sane makes his last stand.'

They stared into each other's drawn faces.

'Desert?' breathed Caine.

'I call it "goin' home". You game?'

Caine's tongue flickered, licking at the rainwater. 'They'll shoot us out of hand if we're caught.'

'You damn fool! We're gonna get shot anyway if we follow this maniac!'

That made sense, but before Caine could reply the decision was taken out of their hands.

There was a sudden commotion. Someone shouted, and it trailed off into a ghastly, gurgling moan that they both recognized as the sound a sentry makes when a knife slashes across his throat in the dark.

This was followed by more shouting, gunfire, screams and curses. Horses whinnied. Musket balls thrummed over their heads. A man burst from the general's tent, tarnished gilt showing on the shoulders of his torn jacket – the general himself! He cried out, shaking a fist at the sodden sky. 'Long live the South!' he hollered as he turned to face his pursuers. Then his body shuddered as half a dozen bullets tore into him, hurling him into the mud.

Crouching behind a bush now, shivering – and not just with cold – the youths watched, wide-eyed and jaw-dropped, as grizzled troopers holding rifles with fixed bayonets rushed through the camp. Three of them stood over the dying general, stabbing repeatedly.

'Where them two boys?' a man with a shaggy, sodden red beard demanded, looking around with staring eyes. 'Crazy Red' Stevens they called him. He claimed he had killed 200 Yankees, wore a pair of dried ears cut from a highly decorated Northern colonel, around his neck, strung on a rawhide thong.'

'Aw, them boys're OK, Red,' said a thick-bodied trooper with a chest-length beard, whom they recognized as a rugged Texan named Mulvaney. 'Told that tow-headed one, Ray, he an' his pard oughta vamoose.'

'You damn fool!' snapped the redhead, menacing with his bloody bayonet. 'They'll blab!'

'Hell, yeah!' growled another veteran, a man from the Mississippi delta, narrow-faced, big-nosed, with a jutting brow. He was a one-time field medic named Campion; word was he had killed more men than he'd saved, both Yankees and Rebs. 'They'll buy their way out of any trouble by sellin' us down the river.'

'Not everyone's the same as you,' said Mulvaney.

'By hell, mister, *you* won't see the end of the war!'

'Them boys done a heap of fightin' for the South, Red. No sense in them dyin' when the war's pract'ly over. They's still only kids and they been good pards.'

'Yeah, Red, Mull's right,' spoke up another trooper. 'They's good boys. I'd like to see 'em get a share of the gold, but if they're already gone, good luck to 'em, I says.'

'We gotta find 'em, damnit!' insisted Campion. 'You cain't trust kids in somethin' like this, Red!'

'Aaaah, we can't stand around here all night,' Red said at last. 'When this wagon don't make the rendezvous on time, the colonel's gonna send all the men he's got lookin' for it. Hell with the kids. Get the wagons rollin' an' we'll start for the Border. Rain'll wash out our tracks.'

Caine and Porteus stayed hidden, mighty tense. Then Mulvaney walked across to their bush and relieved his bladder close by as the wagons started to rumble away. He spoke softly out of the side of his mouth.

'Stay put, boys. Campion's got his blood lust up. Wait'll we get well away before you come out – an' take a look under the ashes of the campfire. Good luck.'

Shivering, teeth chattering, Caine and Porteus lay doggo until the wagons and their murderous outriders drove off into the night. They had hardly faded from sight before Ray Porteus crashed out of the brush and ran towards the remains of the fire.

'Not yet, you damn idiot!' called Caine softly.

'Hell, they're gone. Too interested in makin' the Border to worry about us.' Porteus had his bayonet out, digging frantically into the sodden ashes of the dead campfire. The blade *clunked* on something and he let out a subdued cry, scrabbled with his hands. Caine quickly knelt beside him and helped unearth the booty.

'Hell's teeth!' gritted Porteus. 'It's a bag of double

24

eagles! Good ol' Mulvaney.'

'*Confederate* eagles,' Caine said cautiously. 'Be kinda chancey, the likes of us tryin' to pass 'em at this stage.'

Porteus snorted derisively. 'Gold's gold, ain't it? You think folk are gonna look twice at 'em? Hell, we earned this – we ain't seen a pay in nigh on two years. C'mon, Josh. War's over for us. Let's go see the world – or what's left of it.'

They stayed together through the next ten years. Sharing that bloodstained, ill-gotten gold had made a strong bond between them. Twice they were almost murdered for it, and it was Caine who saved them on each occasion.

The first was at a night camp in the hills above a town called Waylon Springs. Porteus snored in his bedroll but Caine had seen the way two beard-shagged men had looked at them when they had bought supplies for their journey.

He padded his blankets with bundled clothing and gear, placed his battered hat on top so it looked as if he was sleeping there. Then he took his Remington pistol and Spencer carbine – both liberated from dead Yankees at the Battle of the Wilderness – up into the rocks above the camp.

Sure enough, an hour later two shadows came creeping, long knives flashing dully. These men weren't going to give any quarter: they were here to murder the boys in their sleep. So Caine shot them both dead with the Spencer. By that time, Ray was crouching wide-eyed on his own crumpled blanket, fumbling for his pistol.

The next time they were openly held up on the trail.

Three brothers named Wilcox, who had sold them some saddle gear had been stirred by the glint and chink of the remaining gold coins in the chamois poke Caine put back into his jacket pocket after paying.

No words were exchanged as the three brothers sat their mounts, guns menacing, blocking the trail. The eldest Wilcox merely held out his left hand, clicking his fingers in a 'gimme' gesture.

Ray started to argue, always having the gift of the gab and confident he could avert trouble here. But Caine read the men correctly right from the start: gold first, then gunsmoke, was what they had in mind.

So he reversed the order of things: gunsmoke first. He drew his Remington after resignedly nodding, as if he was reaching for the poke of coins. The Wilcoxes grinned in anticipation, the youngest one already lifting his rifle even before they had the gold in their possession.

He was first to die. Caine shot him, held the trigger depressed and chopped at the hammer spur with the edge of his left hand, moving the gun in a short deadly arc. Flame and smoke spurted from the octagonal barrel. He fired all six shots, two each for the brothers, and had started the laborious reloading process with copper powder flask, lead ball, cloth wad, under-barrel rammer, and percussion caps for the chambers, even before the last Wilcox had stopped twitching.

'Where the hell you learn to shoot like that?' demanded Porteus, impressed – not to mention relieved.

Caine shrugged. 'You want to keep your gun where you can reach it quicker, Ray. I could've rolled a cigarette and smoked it before you got it unhitched from your waistband.'

Porteus was about to make a smart remark but stopped, frowning, then nodded gently. 'Foresight caught under the belt edge.' Then he grinned. 'OK, you know what you're talkin' about, I guess, and you're the one got a medal for bravery at Hellfire Crossin'. So I'm makin' you the gunfighter in this deal from now on – an' I'll be the brains. How's that?'

'Sure you can manage it?' Caine gave his easy-going, grin and Ray, who had started to tense up, relaxed. That was how it was as the years passed and they got into and out of scrapes of varying severity: Ray got them into trouble, Caine got them out. The post-war period was mighty turbulent and most men found it all but impossible to make a decent living without breaking at least some of the harsh Reconstruction laws.

So, it wasn't unusual that they weren't always law abiding; mostly they rode a knife edge between legitimate trail jobs. Ray Porteous, who'd been making his way in the world on his own since he was twelve years old, had a yearning for finer things than could be purchased with a cowhand's pay. Caine was surprised to see how well Ray knew his way around small-time illegal practices: throwing an occasional wide loop here and there, slipping contraband back and forth across the Border.

Broke and hungry, they would start a brawl in some town, get thrown in jail for a few days – that gave them a bed and meals. Then, released, they'd go on the drift once again.

They raided an Express office when they were broke, blowing a wall and a safe to hell-and-gone with too much dynamite. Then, just for the hell of it, they attempted to hold up a train, because as Ray said, '*I ain't never tried that before. . . .*'

This time, however, Porteus's plan backfired; they chose a train carrying a posse that had a freight car full of saddled horses, hot on the trail of a notorious outlaw gang.

But the posse was willing to try for the would-be train robbers instead. So they unloaded the eager mounts and went after the fugitives with guns blazing.

The pursuit was so intense that they had to split up. Caine made it safely through the hills, with only a flesh wound across his back, shaking the posse in a rainstorm after three hellish days of dodging lead and hardfaced lawmen, ill-tempered because of the long pursuit.

Ray wasn't so lucky. He was forced to leave his wounded mount and dodge on foot into a nearby town, the posse hard on his heels. There was no easy way to escape. So, in desperation, he stole the sheriff's own horse from outside the law office. In his hurried getaway, he made it look like he took a spill, half a block down the street. He figured it looked pretty authentic, braced himself for the irate lawman. The sheriff pounced, gunwhipped him, and Ray fought back deliberately; he wanted this lawman good and mad at him, so he'd throw him in the cells. Which he did, and where Ray stayed while the posse searched the town for him without success.

The sheriff wanted Ray for himself; not only for

having the hide to steal his horse, but because the young fugitive had given him a bloody nose his deputies were still snickering about. So the sheriff just never mentioned to the posse that he was holding any prisoners in his cell block.

After the posse had gone, Ray figured it hadn't been such a smart move after all. The sheriff was more vindictive than he'd figured and Ray was lucky not to have his neck stretched. Instead, he pulled six months hard-time on the local chain gang, run by the sheriff, making a road and a new pass through the mountains.

'Ain't you fellers heard that slavery's illegal nowadays. . . ?' It was the wrong thing to say and earned Ray a place in the toughest part of the county jail, which in no way resembled a luxury hotel – or even a Mexican flophouse.

He suffered at the hands of some of the inmates, until he palmed a piece of broken glass one day and used it next time someone accosted him. It improved his hard time just a little, but, in that jail, a 'little' was more than welcome.

The sheriff, upon Ray's release, looked at the sunburned, ragged-assed scarecrow standing before him, hat in hand, eyes lowered. 'You'll know better next time not to tangle with me. Now git, an' you ever show your nose in my county again, I'll lock you up and throw the key in the Rio, which happens to be about a hundred miles from here . . . OK?'

Ray couldn't quit town fast enough.

A week later, the sheriff, riding to check a rumour that a wanted outlaw with a big bounty had been seen in canyon country just north of town, was shot from ambush and killed.

The outlaw got the blame, though when he was eventually cornered a month later he emphatically denied he had ever been in that part of the country. He kept up his denials even as they stood him on the gallows.

Ray caught up with a relieved Josh Caine just after he had finished a bronc-busting job for a small outfit in the Cross Hatch Ranges, New Mexico.

He told his story with feeling, and much bitterness.

'That damn sheriff put me through hell! Next time one of us has to do jail, it's your turn. I mean that, Josh! I ain't made to be confined. And I ain't goin' back behind no stone walls ever again.'

Grinning, more pleased to see Porteus again than he wanted to admit, and sorry his pard had been through such hardship, Caine said, 'Was your choice, Ray. Anyway, it did save you from that posse. They'd've likely lynched you.'

'Yeah, mebbe. But I'm tellin' you, Josh – *I ain't goin' back to any jail for no one!* Includin' you.'

Caine made a placating gesture. 'OK, OK, relax. You're out now, and if ever one of us has to do jail time, I'll take my turn if I have to. That make you happy?'

Porteus grinned but insisted they shake hands on it.

Almost a year later, still pards, they came over a gnarled and craggy range at the edge of some badlands one hot sundown, and found themselves in Bear Creek County.

They were broke once again and grub was short; the

coffee beans had been used twice and did little more than colour the water. Ray spat out a mouthful and emptied his mug, swearing.

'Tastes like panther piss!'

'Never had the pleasure – but you might cuss yourself for tossing out that coffee when we're in the middle of the badlands.'

Porteus looked out from the camp halfway up the rise. 'We gotta cross there?'

'According to that pilgrim with the wagon, the town's somewhere over the other side.'

Ray grunted. 'Any baccy?'

Caine tossed him his limp sack. 'Might find a few flakes in the bottom.'

Ray did, and rolled a cigarette that was mostly paper. After a puff he handed it to Caine who took a turn. One more puff from Ray and it was gone.

'We need some *dineros*, pard.'

'Might be some ranch jobs still going,' Caine replied. 'Coupla months yet till fall. We could find ourselves a winter berth in a nice warm bunkhouse with a little luck.'

Porteus curled a lip. 'I'm gettin' kinda tired of forty-and-found, Josh. Growlin' belly most of the time, grub that'd make a billy goat puke, empty pockets. . . .'

'The pilgrim said there were other jobs in town – guard on the stageline, sawmill hand, saloon swamper. . . .'

'I want money in my pocket! Fast!'

'Thought you'd had enough of jail.'

Ray smiled crookedly. 'If a job goes wrong, I ain't the

31

one gonna have to worry about jail time – am I?'

Caine stiffened. 'You gonna hold me to that?'

'We shook on it!' Porteus said shortly, dead serious now. 'You said you'd do the time, Josh!'

Caine frowned. Ray was real stiff about this. 'All right – I said it, so I'll stick by it. But I don't have to worry about it, either. 'Cause we ain't gonna do anything stupid, like rustling cows or trying to rob a train. OK?'

He saw by the fleeting look that crossed Ray's face that it wasn't OK, but Porteus dragged down a deep breath and said, 'OK! Welcher!' He grinned and then stood up, stretching in the crimson glow of the sundown, looking out into the badlands as long shadows crawled across them. 'Hey! Judas priest! There's someone out there! *He's crawlin'!*'

Caine shaded his eyes. 'Yeah – looks plumb tuckered or mebbe hurt. Oh-oh! Riders closing in on him.'

'Well, whoever he is and whatever he's done, he's a goner.' Ray didn't sound very interested and turned away. 'Better douse our fire till they go.'

Caine rounded on him, frowning. 'We can't just. . . .'

Then they heard the first faint rattle of gunfire.

CHAPTER 3

BADLANDS

Ray didn't want to ride down there and find out what was going on.

'Ain't none of our business, Josh. I learned not to poke my nose in where it ain't wanted when I was in jail.'

Caine gave him a cool look as he started to saddle his mount. 'You were with a bunch of men who wouldn't walk across the street to pull a crippled old lady out of the way of a runaway wagon, Ray. Figured you had a better attitude. You helped plenty of strangers during the war.'

'And that never got me nothin' I could use.'

Caine didn't care for this new, surly Ray Porteus; he was willing to make allowances inasmuch as jail had taken its toll, given rise to unusual bitterness, but. . . .

'You want to ride out while I'm down there,' Caine said coldly, with a jerk of his head towards the badlands, 'just take half the grub and leave me my canteen.'

'Hell almighty! You mean that?'

Caine swung into the sadlde. 'Your choice, Ray.'

He wheeled his sorrel and sent it racing down the steep slope, leaving Porteus standing, all agape. Then Ray swore and picked up his saddle.

There were three riders as far as Caine could make out in the dust cloud they were lifting. They were closing fast on the now unmoving man on the ground, two of them shooting. He saw the faint puffs of dust beside the prone man who didn't move. Could be dead already. . . .

Caine spurred his sorrel on, unsheathing the Winchester, thinking once again how he sure could have used such a fine weapon during the war. The men hadn't spotted him yet, concentrating on their quarry. He had deliberately moved around so that he was riding out of part of the sundown's glare and so far it seemed to be working, screening his approach.

One rider on a big black horse rode ahead and came skidding in almost on top of the downed man. He worked his rifle lever and raised the weapon.

Caine fired and the man jerked in the saddle, dropping his rifle and clutching at a blood-spurting arm. He fought to stay up but after some moments toppled out of the saddle. His two pards saw Caine coming out of the sky, firing and triggered their own weapons, their intentions clear enough.

Caine's horse gave a sharp whinny, breaking stride. He carried the Winchester in one hand, dragged at the reins with the other, but couldn't hold the sorrel. A foreleg folded and he didn't wait for gravity to throw him out of leather. He kicked free of the stirrups and jumped. Landing in a crouch, he shoulder-rolled as bullets whistled and spurted dust around him. Going sideways, he triggered one-handed, merely shooting to throw the riders off.

It worked. They veered as he came up on his knees, firing at the one forking the grey. The long-haired rider spun out of the saddle and the other man wheeled away, spurring off, shooting wildly without even trying to aim.

Then Porteus charged in between Caine and his target, forcing him to throw the rifle barrel high. His wasted bullet climbed for the sky. Ray rammed his mount into the other horse and there was a tangle, with the dust cloud full of flailing hoofs and rolling bodies, both men and mounts.

Ray came up out of the cloud and slammed his rifle butt against the head of a rider who was dazed and slow moving. The man dropped and Caine spun as Ray yelled a warning.

The one with the wounded arm was running in on Caine, six-gun in hand now. Caine dropped and the man's boots thudded against his body as the attacker stumbled and fell. Caine kicked out, twisting on to his side. Then he drove his rifle butt against the jaw of the big man.

'Think this one's dead,' Ray said, going down on one knee beside the raider with long black hair whom Caine had shot out of the saddle. 'Wait, mebbe not. No, I think he's just scalp-creased, dammit.'

Caine turned to the one they had first seen crawling. He was groaning now, not really conscious. He wore filthy, ragged clothes, his feet were bare, raw and bleeding from the coarse alkali. His face was bearded, blotched, skin peeling. There were a couple of fresh wounds and bruises that could have been from a fight – or a beating. He was mostly bald on top with a long, ragged, sandy-coloured hair fringe.

'This feller's had it mighty rough.'

Ray turned away from watching the man he had clubbed and who was now showing signs of recovery. He stiffened.

'Them's prison clothes.'

Caine looked more closely at the men they had downed. 'I hope we didn't tangle with a posse.'

Porteus arched his eyebrows. 'That'd be somethin'.'

'Something we could do without.' The clubbed man was sitting up now, holding his head. Caine moved across, prodding him with his rifle barrel; there were no badges showing on vest or shirt. 'What's your interest in the old feller?'

Rheumy eyes travelled up to Caine's face, then swivelled to the unmoving man in rags. 'Who wants to know?'

Caine prodded him again, not gently. 'You were trying to kill him, looked like to me.'

'That so? Well, take some advice, mister; you'd best leave things just as they are. Goddamn! Is Milt dead?'

He was staring at the sprawled, wounded man who had a lot of blood streaking his face.

'Scalp wound. He'll come round soon. I still want to

36

know who you are.'

'Likewise. Why the hell you buy into this?'

'Three riders shooting at a plumb tuckered man on his hands and knees in the badland. Who wouldn't buy in?'

The man was recovering fast now, watched Ray and Caine warily. 'Anyone with enough good sense to wait a spell and see what happened!'

'By then you'd've killed him.'

'Mebbe he needs killin'.'

'Or mebbe you and your pards do.'

The man rubbed his throbbing head. 'Look, that feller busted out of the pen and. . . .'

'Not the Bear Creek jail?' broke in Ray, sounding sceptical.

'Yeah, the one they call the Big Pen.'

Porteus snorted. 'Never happen.'

'You callin' me a liar?'

'Yeah!' Flat and challenging, make what you want of it.

But Caine lifted a hand, stopping Ray's recklessness. 'Don't seem likely an old feller like that could bust out of the Big Pen. No one's ever done it before that I heard.'

'Well, he done it. Someone planted a hoss for him, too, but he run it into the ground an' took off on foot.'

'And you came after him – to kill him.'

The man shook his head, immediately regretted it, grabbed at his temples, smothering a curse. 'Been chasin' the son of a bitch for four days. You want to try it sometime, see how sweet you feel after all that time in

37

the badlands – water sour, grub rotten, hosses actin' up like they come straight outta Hell. Anyway, I was just going to put a couple bullets through his legs, stop him from tryin' anythin' else.'

'You sound mighty miserable to me, mister. That feller's already had some damn rough treatment. You law?'

The man licked his lips. 'Not like you mean. Prison hires us for . . . special jobs.'

'Like running down a tuckered-out old man in the badlands, and when you catch up, beat him up, then try to kill him. How you like me to put a bullet or two through your legs, you son of a bitch!' snapped Caine, lifting his rifle.

The man cringed. 'Don't! I – I was just doin' a job.'

'Miserable way to earn a livin', mister. What're your names?' demanded Ray, prodding hard again.

'I – I'm Kim Barnaby. Feller with the bleedin' arm is Kettle and t'other is Milt Hollis. Why you—?'

'Bind up Kettle's arm, then you and him take Hollis between you and start back the way you came. You can take your canteens but that's all. See how far you can get.'

'Hell's teeth! We'll die out there, without our guns or hosses!'

'Coming on night – it'll be cool walking.' Caine gestured to the ragged man. 'He made it this far on his hands and knees. You ought to do it wearing boots. Or we could make you take 'em off if you give us any more arguments.'

That was enough for Barnaby – he decided to settle

for small mercies.

It was almost dark when the sick and sorry trio stumbled off into the badlands, weaponless.

'We'll see you again, mister!' growled Barnaby.

Ray put a shot into the ground between his boots and then the trio hobbled away, the scalp-creased man's boots dragging and leaving wavering twin lines in the alkali.

Caine watched for a while and then went back to where Ray Porteus was wiping the filthy, bearded face of the old man, now lying on his back. Kneeling, Ray suddenly peered more closely. 'Hey, Josh. Take a look at this!'

Ray opened the stinking shirt and there, resting on the scant grey hairs of the man's pale chest was a pair of shrivelled, mummifed ears, strung on a dark rawhide thong. 'Seen somethin' like this before?'

Caine dropped to one knee and Ray struck a match, holding it close to the bearded, filthy face.

'I don't believe it!'

'It's him all right. Looks like hell – he can't be more'n fifty at most, but you'd take him for seventy.'

Caine had to stare hard but eventually he nodded, recognizing Crazy Red Stevens.

They built up the campfire and set water heating. Caine cut away some of the filth-stiffened clothing, saw the scarred weals from a past whipping – maybe more than one. There were two lumps in the area of his lower ribs and he knew these were the results of bones not knitting properly.

'Well, Red wasn't exactly a sweetie, but the poor devil's been through plenty since we knew him, seems like.'

'Wonder what happened to them gold bars?' Porteus asked, bringing the pan of water and rags torn from the tail of an old shirt. They carefully washed Stevens's battered face, the man moaning and rolling his head from side to side. A quick wash-over of the torso and his back brought more grunts. But while Caine was dabbing the raw flesh dry, Red opened his eyes, which were mattery and caked with grit.

'Can't see . . . who y'are,' he slurred. 'Glare-blind.'

'Close 'em while I wash some of that muck away, Red.' Caine was gentle and Stevens squinted.

'Still cain't – see! Christ, I'm blind!'

'It'll pass,' Caine told him but gave a silent shrug when Ray glanced at him sharply; it wouldn't hurt for Red to believe his sight would return. In truth, Caine had no idea one way or the other.

'You . . . know me. . . ? You called me 'Red'. . . .'

'It's Ray Porteus and Josh Caine, Red. Lieutenant Magill's old squad. . . ?'

'Judas! That was a . . . a long time ago.'

His voice was hoarse and rasping. Porteus dribbled a little more canteen water between the split and peeling lips. Stevens's damaged eyes moved from one man to the other, but he ended up groping with one gnarled hand to feel their presence. 'I can't tell who y'are, but if you've saved my neck, I don't care neither.' He made a cackling sound and the others exchanged a look, Caine shaking his head slowly.

Red was either delirious or half out of his head – permanently – from his time in the penitentiary. Or it could be just too much sun. Or a bad beating. 'What'd you do to get put in the territorial prison, Red?' Caine asked quietly.

Red took his time answering. 'You . . . recollect when we . . . split up?'

'Recollect you seemed fixed on runnin' us through with your bayonet – after you'd done with the general,' Ray said with an edge of bitterness. He ignored Caine's frown.

'Aw, yeah – well, they was hard times. Everyone was actin' kinda crazy.'

'Some were just damn greedy, as I recall,' Ray said, tight-lipped again ignoring Caine's warning gestures; there was no point in harassing Stevens at this stage.

Red made that cackling sound once more. 'Yeah! Gold does that to folk. . . . Gimme more water.' Thirst satisfied, he nodded his thanks as Caine stoppered the canteen. Red wiped his lips with the back of a thin wrist that showed signs of the bone having been broken and never allowed to knit properly; not much medical help in the Big Pen, it seemed.

'You ever make it to Mexico, Red?' Caine asked.

Stevens sobered, shook his head. 'Never did. Yankee patrol jumped us, a whole bunch of 'em. They shot most of the boys, rest of us had no more bullets and had to surrender. Think Campion might've got away—'

'Din' they know the war was over?' Ray sounded indignant.

'Hell, yeah. They knew we were stealin' that gold, too.'

41

'It was Confederate gold, for Chris'sake!'

'Which was lucky for us. They'd've shot us if it'd been Yankee gold. But the damn cap'n said they were havin' a heap of trouble with Reconstruction, local folk not takin' to it – so he decided to put us on trial. Make us look real bad, see? Rebs caught stealin' gold from their own side. But they aimed to punish us accordin' to Reconstruction Law. By that time, was only me an' Mulvaney left.'

'Just a couple no-account Johnny Rebs, eh?' murmured Ray. 'But makin' a big deal out of it. *See what can happen you break Reconstruction Law?* That their idea?'

But Red wasn't listening, bleary eyes looking off somewhere in the gathering night, thoughts a long way from this rough camp on the side of a mountain range in the badlands.

'Judge ordered a firin' squad. Then, last minute reprieve – gave us "life" instead. Life *imprisonment*! I'd rather've had a bullet!'

'Mighty rough, Red,' Caine allowed. 'Dunno how you managed to survive this long. Mulvaney make it?'

The mattery eyes swung in Caine's direction slowly. 'You might say that. He's still in the Pen.'

'How come?' Ray asked suspiciously.

' 'Cause he was locked up in solitary when the chance come for me to get out.'

'And you took it.'

'Damn right! *You* wouldn't've lasted ten weeks in there, sonny. Me, I've been there best part of ten *years*. I didn't aim to die in there – like Mulvaney.'

42

Caine stiffened. 'You said he was still alive.'

'Oh, sure – as alive as anyone can be in solitary.'

'You left him!'

'Don't git on your high hoss. You got no idea what it's like in there. You'd leave your own mother behind if the chance come to escape an' you knew she'd only slow you down or get you caught.'

Caine signed to Ray. 'We dunno how it was, Ray.'

'You mightn't, but I got some idea. I guess I can savvy you goin' it alone, Red. But ol' Mulvaney was always good to me and Josh. Too bad he's gonna end up like that.'

'Bein' soft-hearted makes you soft in the head,' Stevens said flatly. 'But don't get the notion that ol' Mull was always all sweetness an' light.'

'What're you talking about?'

'We was passin' through some mighty rugged mountains, well south of here, with that wagon of gold. I woke up one night an' seen Mull's bedroll was empty. He din' show up again for a day an' a half, lookin' plumb tuckered.'

Ray frowned. 'Where'd he been?'

Red almost smiled. 'Forgot to say he'd took one of the mules with him. He never brought it back.'

Ray's frown deepened but Caine said quietly, 'He took some of the gold – that what you're saying?'

Red nodded, mouth tight enough to squeeze a drop of blood from one of the splits in his lips. 'Yeah. Ten bars, each one weighin' about eight pounds. Worth near twenty thousand bucks now.'

'Peanuts to what that wagon was carrying, Red.'

'Mebbe – but it weren't his to take! I jumped him about it, and the others backed me, but all he'd say was, "Take it outta my share. Not tryin' to rob no one. Just want somethin' stashed away before we get caught an' lose the lot".'

'Playing it safe.'

'He kept sayin' it was for somethin' "special" . . . I knew if I OK'd it, the others'd be wantin' to take their shares, too, and I couldn't allow that. Russ Campion was ready to kill Mull, mean sonuver when it comes to money is Russ. But I told Mull he better go fetch it back and pronto. Was about then that the Yankee patrol jumped us.'

'Those ten bars are still wherever Mull took them?' Ray asked tautly, his words bringing a frown to Caine's face.

'Reckon so. He never said where he hid 'em.' He shook his head slowly. 'I been tryin' for ten years just to get him to tell me. Hell, I mean, I was in no position to go steal 'em, I was just curious – but he might just as well've sewed his lips together for all he told me about 'em.'

'And now you're out,' Ray said, eyes sparkling some in the firelight. 'But you must've picked up a couple of clues in ten years where he might've stashed 'em!'

Red glanced at him, but whether he could see or not was something else. 'Now who's feelin' greedy?'

Ray's face straightened. 'Not a matter of greed – just common sense. The gold ain't doin' Mulvaney any good while he's in the pen. Nor anyone else!'

'It's still his – as much as anyone's,' Caine pointed out.

'Yeah, "as much as anyone else's", like you just said. That means us right now! If Red here'll tell us where he thinks it is . . . I mean, we just saved his neck an'—'

'How the hell would I know? I already told you, Mull wouldn't say.'

'But you know where you were when Mull took off with the gold, and he was only gone just over a day. You know somethin', Red, that's why you busted out, ain't it!'

'How did you bust out?' asked Caine, interested.

Red's face blanked out. 'Mull always said there had to be a way out, but I dunno if he ever found it, he spent most of his time in solitary. But I had a little help from the jail sawbones – an ol' friend. Gimme a potion to make me sick. Had to go to the infirmary. He fixed it from there.'

Ray was on his feet now, excited. 'You tried to crawl across the badlands! You were goin' after them gold bars!'

Red Stevens lay back and closed his eyes. 'You want to know about them bars, go get yourself a cell in solitary next to Mulvaney. I ain't sayin' another thing.'

'Well, mebbe we can change your mind for you!'

'Ray! Put your gun away, dammit! How the hell did we get into this? Ride down to help someone, now you're getting ready to kill him!'

'Not till he tells me where to find the gold!' Ray was simmering, his hand still on his six-gun, glaring at Josh Caine. 'You don't have to buy into this!'

'I damn well do – and I am.'

'Listen! Durin' the War, Red was rough as a cob on

45

us because we were a couple of kids, bullied the hell outta us, give us all the trash jobs, rubbed our noses in it. Now, we got him where we can bully *him* a little.'

'Looks to me like he's had a goin'-over. Barnaby and his friends, Red. . . ?'

Red said nothing and Ray scowled.

'He wouldn't've risked his neck bustin' out if he didn't think he could turn up that gold.'

'Good reasonin', mister,' a voice said out of the darkness. 'Just what we was thinkin', too.'

The three of them appeared at the edge of the flickering firelight: Kim Barnaby, Kettle, with his wounded arm crudely bandaged now, and Milt Hollis, the edge of a dirty rag showing beneath his hat. They all had guns.

'Son of a *bitch*!' Ray murmured. 'They doubled back in the dark!'

'We ain't quite finished with Red yet,' Barnaby said. 'See, there was four of us originally. But Luke's hoss snapped a leg out there in the badlands, threw him on to some rocks and killed him. We was kinda anxious to catch up with Red so we pushed on – left Luke an' his rifle and the two six-guns he always wore. We recollected where we'd left him, after you kicked us out, so we went an' found the place again; and now we got you flat-footed!'

'It only looks that way,' Caine said and, on the last word, his Colt came up blasting. Ray threw himself to one side, skidding across the ground to where his rifle rested. It still had a shell in the breech and he snatched the gun and triggered, hard on the heels of Caine's second shot.

The trio scattered but Milt Hollis only took two steps before crumpling and sliding away down the slope. Kim Barnaby moved the fastest, shooting as he twisted away. Then Ray's rifle bullet caught him in the shoulder and spun him like a top. He went down, trying to bring his Colt across his body, even as Ray shot him through the head.

Caine was down on one knee, beading Kettle as the man ran downslope into the darkness. The six-gun roared and bucked twice against his wrist. Kettle was punched forward until his legs went from under him. He skidded several yards on his face before coming to a halt.

Caine, still crouching, ramming out the used shells and reaching for replacements in his belt, turned to look at Ray who was kneeling beside Red Stevens.

'OK?'

Ray looked up, face grim in the firelight. 'I am, but Red's stopped a bullet.'

Caine, closing the Colt's cylinder, looked steadily at Ray. 'There goes your plans for getting your hands on that gold, then.'

Ray met and held his gaze. 'Aw, I dunno. That sawbones must've thought Red knew somethin' or he wouldn't't've helped him bust out: and Red ain't quite dead yet.'

'For Chris'sake, Ray! What's wrong with you? No one's gonna get them bars. Quit dreaming about it.'

'You heard what Red said. "Get yourself into a cell next to Mulvaney". . . .' He jabbed his Colt's barrel

47

suddenly into the dying man, making him moan, catch his breath. 'Means he thinks Mull can still tell where the bars are. That's right, ain't it, Red?'

Stevens moaned sickly, barely conscious.

'Leave him be!' snapped Caine, his hand still resting on the holstered six-gun. 'The hell's gotten into you?'

'Nothin' that wasn't there all along!' Ray told him, tight-faced. 'I'm tired of half-starvin' between jobs that don't pay enough to buy me a warm coat for winter. Tired of *takin' orders*! All them years in the army, bein' pushed around, then gettin' the liver kicked outta me in jail if I was a hair slow obeyin' an *order*! Now the same thing tryin' to earn a livin': more goddamn *orders*! Straighten that fencepost, cowboy; pull that wire taut; heat that brandin' iron more; hurry up an' shoe that bronc – you got rheumatics. . . ? Do this, do that, or draw your time! Judas priest, Josh, I've had me a bellyful! When I got outta jail, I promised myself if ever a chance come for me to make easy money, lawful or not, I was gonna grab it – hell or high water.'

'And now you think it's time,' Caine said quietly.

'Damn right'. Now it's come, an' I'm gonna grab it with both hands!' His eyes were hard in the firelight as he bored his gaze into Caine. 'And you're gonna help me.'

CHAPTER 4

ROAD AGENT

Red Stevens died without regaining consciousness. They buried him by himself, but put the others in a common grave. It was hot, exhausting work even by moonlight, and afterwards they were almost too tired to make supper.

But they stirred the fire and, in silence, brewed weak coffee, heated beans and stale corn dodgers. Sand-scrubbing the plates after they had eaten, before rinsing them with a minimum of water, Caine felt Porteus staring at him. He glanced over his shoulder.

'It's still no,' he said flatly.

'You shook hands on it!'

'OK. Now I'm welching.' Caine paused, the inference being that Ray could make of that what he wanted and if he felt he had to do something about it then now was the time. 'I said I'd do jail time if some hare-brained scheme we thought up went wrong. But that was local jail time we were talking about and you know it. Not serious time in a penitentiary.'

'You said you'd do it. No mention of local hoosegows or otherwise.' Ray was sullen now, a kind of mood that had been more obvious and frequent since he came off the chain gang. 'Hell, it wouldn't be for long – just get next to Mulvaney and find out what we need to know. If Mull don't know of a way out like Red said, see the sawbones. We can give him a small cut if he helps you.'

'You want to know what I think, Ray? I reckon you fell and hit your head, or one of them chain gang warders banged it too damn hard with his billy and it's addled your brain. You're talking like a half-wit kid.'

'You son of a bitch!'

Ray's rage almost choked him and he was moving on the first word, leaping across the fire and swinging the old skillet he had been scrubbing. Caine threw up an arm instinctively and grunted as the iron utensil banged against his limb. He lowered it hurriedly, ducked under Ray's second swing, and came up inside the man's guard.

He ripped two fast blows into Porteus's midriff and Ray staggered back, the skillet dropping to his side. Caine kicked it from his grip, drove a punch at Ray's jaw. It clipped him on the point and he went down to one knee, blinking, shaking his head.

Then he launched himself forward. Caine was on the downhill side of the slope and Porteus'a body took him high so that he overbalanced. Locked together, they rolled and skidded down the slope, dust rising around them. They tried to punch and elbow each other but couldn't release their grips for long. They tumbled on to a flatter section and Ray got a knee into Caine's belly. Josh grunted, his grip loosened, their bodies separated. Caine lashed out with a leg, his boot catching Ray as he started up to hands and knees. Ray's head snapped back and he slid down another few feet.

Caine, dragging in a deep breath, staggered upright. One boot slipped and he stumbled again and straightened at the same time as Ray. Their eyes met.

They both went for their guns.

Caine was faster – he was always the faster of the pair – and Ray blanched, freezing in a crouch, his gun not quite clear of leather, as Caine cocked his hammer.

He saw the fear in Ray's eyes as the knowledge that he was about to die reached his brain.

Blood on his face, Caine started to lift his thumb from the hammer spur; suddenly he stopped and pressed down hard, holding the gun at full cock.

'God almighty! What the hell're we doing!' Caine said breathlessly, lowering the hammer now and letting his gun arm drop to his side. He shook his head. 'I damn near killed you, Ray!'

Ray Porteus released a long, shuddering breath, blinked, and let his Colt fall back into the holster. He cleared his throat.

'I *know*!' His voice cracked and he gusted one more deep breath, than sat down, rubbing his throbbing jaw. He glanced up and there was still a wariness in his look. 'An' I was tryin' to kill you. But I knew I was gonna be too slow.' He wiped beads of sweat from his dusty brow. 'Man, I don't want to go through that again.'

51

Caine's face was very sober. 'That'd be up to you.'

Ray snapped his head up, eyes blazing briefly, then he nodded gently. 'OK. I pushed it. I was a damn fool. We pards again?'

Caine's face or stance didn't change for a moment. Then he visibly relaxed and grinned crookedly as he held out his right hand.

They turned in and Caine was just settling into his bedroll when Ray said quietly,

'There's still a way to do it, you know. . . .'

Caine swore, hurled a boot in the direction of Porteus's voice and heard Ray chuckle as he fended it off.

'Go to sleep!' Caine growled.

'OK. And I'll dream up somethin' that'll change your mind.'

They stopped their dusty, weary mounts at the edge of the boardwalk outside the stage depot. Men and horses were coated with a fine film of alkali.

Ray grinned through his white mask and gestured at the sun-weathered handbill pinned to the clapboard wall beside the entrance.

'Still there. Now *that* has to be a good sign.'

Caine thumbed back his hat and shook his head slowly. 'Well, I sure didn't think that job'd still be going. It took us two days to cross the badlands. Could be it's too dangerous, Ray, and no one wants it.'

Porteus was already dismounting, called to a man who was pinning up a stage schedule near the other notice.

'Shotgun guard's job still goin'?'

'That's what it says.' The man didn't bother turning around.

'Been goin' for some while, ain't it?'

'So?'

'Why? Somethin' wrong? Piddlin' pay? Too many road agents. . . ?'

The man turned now and looked at Ray, spared a brief glance at Caine, still sitting his horse, all covered with alkali. 'Come across the badlands, huh? There's only the one job.'

'Only one of us applyin',' Ray told him.

'You rode shotgun before?'

'No. But I've drove a stage.' Ray lied easily. 'Southline, Arizona. I've met my share of road agents.'

The man was squat, curly-haired. He hauled at his trousers which tended to slip over his barrel belly. He wrinkled his rubbery nose. 'I'm the agent. I hire and fire.' He hesitated, then said, 'Look, we had a man – two days back. He was shot when a drunken cowhand wanted to hitch a ride on a full stage. Ain't been a hold-up down this way in a coon's age, but we got a run comin' up with a strongbox, and I need a man in a hurry. S'pose I up the pay a mite? You be interested?'

'Hell, I'm your man.'

The stage agent glanced at Caine but he was already riding slowly away. 'Might find somethin' at the sawmill, mister,' the agent called, but Caine didn't turn.

Ray tied his mount's reins loosely round the rail and stretched. 'How about we talk money?'

'Come on in. Name's Jack Wall.'

53

'Chad Wilson,' Ray said without hesitation, smiling. 'Man, I'm sure lookin' forward to bein' able to afford a beer to wash this damn alkali outta my throat.'

'Reckon I can find somethin' in the office bottle. That friend of yours don't seem too friendly.'

Ray shrugged, not even glancing at Caine as he rode out into the Main Street traffic. 'Just someone I met comin' in across the alkali. Company, you know? He was half-starved, so we shared my last strips of jerky.'

Jack Wall looked closely at Ray. 'Good to see a man who'll help another out when he needs it.'

'Dunno no other way. Er, can I help you locate that bottle?'

Agent Wall laughed. 'No need. Know just where it is!'

'You din' have to run off like that.'

Caine, sitting with his back against the wall of a store shed in an alley behind Main, shrugged.

'Didn't want him to get too good a look at me.'

Ray smiled, clapped him on the shoulder. 'So. You're gonna do it?'

Caine sighed, looked reluctant. 'I . . . guess so. It's not what I had in mind, Ray. I'm damned if I want to go on the run again, but . . . you're right. We need a stake in a hurry so we can get right away from this damn country, head north to somewhere green. Hear Wyoming or Montana are good.'

'If you don't mind freezin' your balls off. But, yeah, we can find somewhere there ain't so much dust to clog a man's lungs. Gulf Coast, mebbe. Be a lot easier if we had about twenty thousand to back us up.'

Caine's face straightened. 'I thought we'd settled that.'

'Yeah, yeah, OK. Just a thought. Hate to think of them gold bars sittin' there sinkin' into the ground, not doin' no one any good, though.'

'Might be a good haul in this strongbox. Did the agent say?'

'Didn't want to push my luck by asking. All I know is it's bound for the Totem copper mine, which has about fifty men workin' for it!'

Caine smiled despite himself. 'Let's hope it's a month's payroll.'

Ray grinned. 'Be nice, huh? I make a trial run tomorrow on an ordinary passenger stage up to Curtis Bend and back. The strongbox run's the day after. I've got a map of the route but you'll have to go scout out the best place. By the way, Jack Wall asked about you an' I said your name was Frank Keller, and we'd met in the badlands.'

'Frank Keller. OK. Did you get an advance on your pay?'

'Ten bucks was all he'd spring to, told me to get some decent clothes. I can spare you five.'

Caine nodded; that would see him through overnight and buy him a grubsack so he could ride out and pick a good spot to hold up the stage.

With the shotgun guard being in on the deal, it ought to be a cinch.

It wasn't – and Caine didn't know for sure just what went wrong.

He left his horse well out of sight in a draw where there was enough grass for the animal to browse on and stay put. His story was to be that it had thrown him and run off – which was why he was afoot and flagging down the stage.

It would be up to Ray to convince the driver that they ought to stop and pick up a lone man out here. Then Caine would get the drop on both driver and guard, tell them to throw down their guns and the strongbox. Afterwards, he'd order them to cut the team loose.

Now, standing on the small slope, watching the stage approach ahead of a roiling cloud of dust, he could see Ray talking animatedly to the driver. The tobacco-chewing stage man eventually hauled on the reins. He saw the man gesture to Ray's shotgun, still on the floor at their feet. Ray took his time about reaching for it.

But he stood up without the gun as the stage rocked to a halt, a couple of passengers looking curiously out of the windows. As the dust started to clear and Caine reached for his gun a rock turned under one boot and he stumbled, lost balance and sprawled.

'Get your goddamn gun!' the driver shouted, his voice cracking in rising fear. 'It's a hold-up!'

'Nah, I don't think so.' Ray stalled, squinting, hanging on to the seat rail, straining to see better. 'He fell'

'Judas priest! *Get your Greener for Chris'sakes*! Before he gets up!'

The grizzled driver was looking at this new guard strangely and Ray knew he had to at least reach for the gun; the driver was already suspicious.

When Caine got to his feet, inwardly cursing, he found himself looking into the muzzles of the sawed-off shotgun. He flicked his gaze upwards and Ray stared at him, grimfaced, above the weapon. *Right into his role as the stage guard earning his pay. . . .*

'Lift 'em, mister! We got you dead to rights!' Ray rolled his eyes towards the driver and the passengers who were now talking and gesturing excitedly. 'We're all witnesses that you tried to hold up this coach!'

'I was flagging you down for a lift!' Caine protested, frowning at Ray. 'Horse run off, left me stranded. I'm no road agent.'

'Tell it to the sheriff, feller,' growled the driver. 'Whoo-ee! Thought I was gonna see some shootin' for the second time in a coupla days. Was my stage that drunk cowpoke held up an' shot the other guard.' He looked soberly at Ray. 'You were kinda slow, by the way, Wilson.'

Ray shrugged. 'New to this. Didn't want to get into a shoot-out first day out if I could help it.'

'Then why the hell you take the job?'

'Man has to eat.' Ray turned hard eyes on Caine. 'This one looks like he'll be headin' for the Big Pen.' Caine stiffened and Ray smiled crookedly. 'They tell me Judge Cobb just loves sendin' outlaws there.'

'I'm no outlaw.'

'Reckon we could've made a mistake, Banjo?'

The driver snorted. 'What you expect him to say? No, you're right. He's bound for the Big Pen for sure.'

Ray's and Caine's glances locked. 'Maybe I'll have a different story to tell. Could be I'll get nothing but a rap over the knuckles.'

Ray laughed. 'You're dreamin'. You hear him, Banjo?'

'I hear the son of a bitch. Mister, we *know* what we saw and we'll tell it like it happened. You're a goner.'

'Better get used to the idea, feller. You're done for. We make our story hard enough, you could see the gallows.'

'I should've left you in the badlands,' Caine said coldly, recognizing Ray's veiled threat.

'You know this sonuver?' Banjo asked in surprise.

'We crossed the badlands together. Wouldn't say I know him. Just well enough to bet he don't like the idea of goin' to the Bear Creek Pen.'

'Damn right I don't, and could be—'

'Aw, don't make such a fuss. Look on it as a . . . what? A sort of holiday, a break from all that stress tryin' to dodge the law for robbin' our stage. Never know who you might meet in there. Find someone who knows the ropes – could see you spend the time . . . profitably.'

Caine knew damn well what Ray was saying; it might not have been planned this way, but now Ray saw the chance to do what he'd wanted all along: *Get Caine into the Big Pen and alongside Mulvaney.* And Ray didn't aim to pass it up.

As Ray saw it, the only problem would be getting Caine out again so they could go collect those gold bars. But he would worry about that part later.

It was Caine's biggest problem, too, because he knew there was no way he wouldn't see the inside of the Big Pen now. Ray, with the help of Banjo and the passengers, would make sure he was railroaded there direct. A double-cross by chance . . . or was it something Ray had planned all along when he had first suggested the stage hold-up while he was riding shotgun?

He had thought it was a quick turnaround on Ray's part; now he was damn sure Ray had seen a chance to get Caine into the Big Pen and next to Mulvaney by playing his part as shotgun guard and preventing the 'hold up' from taking place, capturing the road agent to make it look good – for himself.

'*Just doin' my job, Mr Wall, sir*. . . .'

And about all that Caine *could* do was to make the most of it, now.

And settle with Ray Porteous once he got out.

If he got out.

CHAPTER 5

DEVIL'S HOLE

So here he was, finally, in solitary. It's nickname was well-chosen: the 'Devil's Hole'. It could be a hole in a corner of hell: pitch black, silent, detached from the rest of the world. A waiting room – *for what?*

For the kind of private hell such a place could conjure up in a man's mind if he was left there long enough, alone with his own demons whirling in his mind.

They left Caine without food or water for two days. On the third morning, in the sludgy grey light that filtered down through the dirt-smeared high window, a flap was opened in the bottom of the door. A thin blanket was pushed through, followed by a bowl of some revolting mush and a cup of something luke-warm and odourless that he supposed was coffee.

'How about a spoon?'

'How about you shut your mouth. No talkin' – an' no

spoons or knives.'

'Slop bucket?'

'Aw, Mack, we done forgot his bucket.'

'Tut-tut. I'll never forgive meself for such an oversight. Damn! I know I won't sleep tonight now.'

Their laughter faded as the flap was closed. He picked up the bowl of slop and began to shovel it into his mouth with his fingers.

His stomach rebelled but he managed to keep it down. It left such a foul taste in his mouth that he gulped down half the 'coffee' before he realized it tasted mighty salty.

About twenty minutes later he knew that this was caused by the addition of a strong dose of Epsom Salts. . . .

No wonder the sons of bitches had 'forgotten' his slop bucket! Their idea of 'fun'. . . .

So that was the way it was going to be in the Devil's Hole.

The half-light annoyed him. Not that the small rock cubicle was worth exploring – a single sweep of the eyes was enough to take in all its drabness and squalor. But what got to him more than he had expected it to, was the silence. The walls were thick and so was the door.

No outside noise filtered in: it was as if there was no one else left in the world.

He wondered how long it would be before they brought him another meal. Not that he looked forward to the grey slop itself, but to hear the scrape of the flap and the clatter of the bowl and cup on the tray – and even the cursing insults of the guards. . . .

All part of the plan, he guessed. Isolation – solitary in the full sense of the word.

No choice, he settled down to accept it. Starvation diet. The only drink available was the laxative 'coffee'. Deprived of sound and the basic human comforts. Live with the stench of his own body waste. . . .

He could take it – but for how long? He had deliberately attacked prison guards. He had been badly beaten for it, but he knew that that wasn't the end of it. He had bucked the system and he'd be made to pay for it.

Hell almighty! He wasn't sure he could take it!

'Who's in there?'

His heart shot up into his throat and goosebumps prickled all over his body. Dry-mouthed he said, tentatively, 'Who said that?'

'Name's Mulvaney.' The voice sounded harsh, weak. Caine shook his head: was he dreaming? 'Where the hell are you?'

'Next door. You got Devil's Hole Two – I'm in One. Reserved for the real bad boys. I've spent years on and off in your cell, but I been upgraded now.' He chuckled. 'Don't ask why.'

'How the hell can I hear you? There's a solid stone wall between.'

There was a faint chuckle that deteriorated into a bout of coughing, followed by painful-sounding wheezes.

Groping his way along the wall, feeling for some kind of opening, Caine asked, 'You OK, Mull. . . ?'

'N-no!' The single word was grunted with hard

effort, and the wheezing faded. He heard gasping at about the same time as his fingers touched the edge of a hole maybe four inches square: space for a removable brick.

'I . . . ain't OK. I'm dyin'. Ticker's actin' up, got lung . . . fever. Don't think I'll . . . be gettin' outta here – this time. . . .'

'Mull – it's Josh Caine. From Magill's squad. You recall me and Ray Porteus. . . ?'

Mulvaney took his time answering, his breathing hard and ragged, making whistlings and whines and crackles that ended in another fit of coughing.

'Mother Mary an' Joseph. *Someone's* heard my prayers. I been needin' . . . someone I can . . . trust. How the hell you get here, boy?'

'Long story, Mull.'

'You got someplace to go?'

'Like to have – anywhere outta here'll do.'

'How you got *in* is what I wants to know.'

So Caine told him, his mouth dry by the time he had finished, but he was damned if he was going to take even one more sip of that Epsom Salts drink.

'So Ray double-crossed you. Turned that piss-ant hold-up right around an' got you in here like he wanted all along. Well, I always had him figured as the sneaky one of you pair. An' it's all so you can find out from me what I done with them gold bars?'

'Ten of 'em, Red said.'

'Six, I took . . . someone else got the other four before me. Campion, I reckon. But I got the blame for takin' the lot. Don't make no difference now.'

63

There was more coughing. 'I . . . need . . . to . . . rest up . . . a little. I'll put the . . . brick back in. Talk later. . . .'

'I'd like to keep talking. The silence gets to me.'

There was an odd sound that might have been a croaking laugh. 'It does that. I've spent most of the . . . ten years I been in this dump in and outta . . . these . . . hell-holes. Done a . . . lotta work . . . but it ain't gonna do me . . . no good now.'

'C'mon, Mull! You was never one to give up. Plenty of times you got Ray an' me through some damn nightmare battle by urging us never to give up.'

'You was . . . just . . . boys. Needed someone to . . . help you . . . through. Josh – gimme a l'l time . . . boy. I . . . I'll have . . . to put the brick . . . in . . . for now. . . .'

'Well, you rest easy, Mull. I'll be here.'

And a fat lot of good I'll be in here when he's ailing beyond the stone wall! Caine thought – but under the circumstances, it was the best he could do.

He dozed. Stomach cramps woke him. He was parched but emptied out the remains of the 'coffee' in case thirst got the better of him. He felt his way back to his corner near the loose brick and sat with his legs drawn up, head resting on his arms folded on his bent knees.

There was no notion of time passing, except he was served one more meal of the awful pig-slop, and a cup of untainted water. Maybe it was a whole day had passed; he had no way of knowing. The guards refused to speak and Mulvaney hadn't touched the brick. Caine had tried to push it out from his side but it wouldn't move.

There was nothing he could do but wait, doze, waken, and wait some more, till sleep overtook him once again. *God, he hoped Mulvaney hadn't died in his cell!*

The light and that awful silence was just the same when he opened his eyes once more. Except – the silence had been broken by a brief scraping sound. *Food!* No, this came from the wall near his head. A faint grey square showed a couple of feet from where he sat.

'Mull? Feeling any better?'

'Some. Hard to tell, Josh. Queer sensations in my chest an' arms. Kind of a tinglin', like a cold numbness. . . .'

Caine tensed. His mother had said something similar just before she had the stroke that eventually took her life.

'Wish I could do something to help you, Mull.'

'Ah. You always was soft-hearted. Not like Ray. Recollect you rescuin' a cat from house rubble after a cannonade. Nursed it back to health, fed and carried it in your pack, till it got drowned on a river crossin'. Campion said he'd eat it and you pinned his hand to the ground with a bayonet, buried the cat yourself. Ever you meet Russ again, boy, he'll recollect that day, too – but for different resons.'

'Hell with Russ Campion. My worry is being stuck here.'

'Thanks to that little son of a bitch, Ray, huh?'

'Aw, he's not so bad. Had it rough a year or so ago. Sheriff named Larson got his hooks into him and—'

'Don't tell me! Larson's chain gang! Well known, even in here. Wouldn't've done him any good, but

65

never mind. You know what he's like. Just don't drop your guard.'

Caine snorted. 'Think I already did. Otherwise I wouldn't be here.'

Silence, except for Mulvaney's laboured breathing. It seemed to drag on for long minutes.

'Josh – I've had time to sort some things out in my mind. I've done some bad things in my life, a few good ones, too, but . . . I doubt they balance out. But what's worried me for too many years is: I was a drunk. A fightin' drunk. The booze took a lot outta me and I was too dumb to notice till I started losin' most of the fights I got into.' He paused and Caine heard him swallow before continuing: 'So then, for my own self-respect, I had to pick fights I knew I could win. . . .'

Caine was suddenly aware he was holding his breath: *he knew what was coming.*

'God help me! I started pickin' on my own family!' The words were flung out now, gasped, rather than spoken 'My wife. My . . . daughter . . . an' my son. I only ever beat up once on him, then he took off. Never seen him again. Don't even know if he's still alive. Then *I* took off, too. Ran out and left my wife and daughter to fend for themselves.'

Caine frowned and moved uncomfortably; it sounded like Mulvaney was . . . crying now. Or trying damn hard not to.

'My father used to beat us, too. Ma, me, younger sister. But Ma lit out with us kids. Worked herself to death to rear us. Never knew what happened to the old man.'

'Aw, Josh! I'm afraid somethin' like that might've happened to my wife and daughter. Started lookin' for 'em once but the war came an' I was in trouble. Joined the army to dodge it, an'. . . .' Then, abruptly he stopped speaking, and there was another long pause.

'All right! That's enough of that. What I'm leadin' up to is . . . I'll tell you what I done with the gold, 'cause I always felt you could be . . . trusted an' I ain't gonna be able to do anythin' about it myself now.' A long pause, punctuated by slow, heavy breaths. 'I want your word first that if you find it, you'll give half to my family – or whoever's still livin'. If you really can't find 'em – it's all yours.'

Caine blew out his lips. 'You got my word, but that's a lot of responsibility, Mull!'

'You can handle it, Josh. Would never ask . . . Ray.' He stopped again and Caine heard a sudden intake of breath and a small moan.

He pressed his hands flat against the stone wall, placed his mouth into the opening. 'Mull! Mull, are you OK?'

More moans and gasps and what sounded like some scrabbling or writhing. *Jesus, he's having an attack! Dying!*

Then: 'Ugh! Bad one, boy. Reach through far as you can.' Caine forced his arm into the hole as far as he could, felt Mulvaney's calloused fingers as the man pushed something into his hand. It felt like a – big nail! 'I – I got me a real wild head of . . . hair now. I pick up all the dead bugs . . . I can find, stash 'em in it.'

'The hell for?'

A half-laugh: 'Keeps the guards from searchin' for

stuff like . . . that . . . nail. Had it four years . . . now. What . . . what I dug the brick out with.'

'I hope I'm not still here in four years!'

Another suggestion of a laugh. 'No, boy. You can be outta here in . . . in a couple hours . . . long as it's dark . . . outside.'

'How can I—'

'Your window. When you can't see . . . its outline . . . you know it's night. No other way to tell from in here. . . .'

'I meant, how can I get outta *here*? It's like being buried.'

'Just like . . . that.' There was a strangled sort of sound and Caine's voice was panicky as he called Mull's name. 'Just . . . another hard . . . pain . . . I gotta talk . . . not much time . . . don't interrupt. . . .'

Caine pressed his ear to the hole, taking in everything Mulvaney told him: count four floor-stones out from the hinge side of the door, and four out from the wall on the same side as the hinges. Use the nail to scratch the filling from around the two flagstones that this'll locate. Prise them up. The hole should be large enough for his shoulders: might have to lose a layer of skin, but squeeze on down. Feel on the side of the hole nearest the door – a small tin half-buried in the earthen wall. The waterproof tin holds a few vestas and a map drawn in charcoal showing where the gold is stashed.

'The dragon'll take care of it till you get there.'

Caine thought Mull's mind must be wandering with the pain. 'What dragon, Mull? Ain't they just . . . myths?'

He felt the rough hand clawing into the hole, reached back and touched it: there wasn't enough room for a proper grip.

'Don't 'spect wife to still be alive – Bertha. But daughter should be – Eve. After my . . . Ma. . . .'

'Hell, Mull, where do I start looking?' *Provided I can get out of here.*

'On . . . map . . . Josh, that hole in there. Dig down two feet. There's another shaft under. Place is built over an old well; it was a Spanish monastery once. Monks done penance . . . locked in . . . these here cells. There's water at bottom of shaft, 'bout ten feet down. It flows somewheres underground. Checked what I could in the library . . . b'lieve it joins Bear Creek.'

'But you don't *know?*'

'Monks used to lower themselves into the water, half-drown themselves as punishment for their imagined sins. Don't really know where it goes but it's your only chance. I . . . I can't even . . . swim. Too late for me, anyway. But you can use it, boy. You . . . gotta!'

Caine wasn't enthusiastic about this. 'Red Stevens said a doctor helped him, with some sort of drug. Sounded a helluva lot easier than going down this well.'

'Doctor my ass. He visits the pen sometimes, "good will" he reckons. Calls hisself "Doctor" Russell, but he's Russ Campion. Still dunno much more medicine than when he was a field medic. He's after the gold; that's why he helped Red get out – thought he knew where it is. Red musta led him on, 'cause I never told Red anythin' much. Workin' on me now. Holdin' back my . . . heart medicine, tryin' to get me to talk but— Aw!

Oh, *Christ*! *J-Josh! I – I'm done*!'

The fingers convulsed once, then went suddenly limp, were withdrawn, and though Caine called Mulvaney's name several times there was no answer – only hacking coughs and groans – and the scrape of the brick being pushed back into place.

Just before it filled the hole, there was a final brief gasping, almost unintelligible:

'Luck . . . boy!'

CHAPTER 6

ONE WAY OUT

He figured that Mulvaney had pushed the brick back from his side so that when they discovered the old man's body there would be no sign that there had been any communication through the wall. If they thought Caine and Mulvaney had talked they would immediately check on Caine's cell.

But making the brick less noticeable would delay the discovery that Caine had escaped – or, leastways, had *tried* to. For once he got into that well shaft it would be all or nothing; there would be no way back. And what lay ahead was anybody's guess.

There was dullness in his cell – he couldn't really call it any kind of light. But running his fingers along the wall, he could feel the small gap around this end of the brick. With a lantern it would stand out. He ought to try to fill it in with something – but what?

While the greyness lasted, he located the two

flagstones side by side on the floor according to Mulvaney's instructions. There was some sort of grimy fill around the edges. It didn't feel like cement or mortar. Maybe some substitute Mulvaney had used when he had first found out about the well beneath Number Two cell's floor. How he'd done it, he didn't know, but the old Texan had been a reader in the army. If this hellish place ran to a library of some kind Mull would have made what use of it he could. Anyway, that wasn't important.

He took the three-inch nail – well worn – and began to dig at the filling. It was difficult at first but he soon discovered there was just a hard crust on top and it was kind of like stale dough underneath. Breathing faster than normal – excitement and tension making his arms ache – Caine worked his way around the flagstones. It was pitch black by the time he had finished.

He jumped about a foot in the air, he reckoned, when the food flap scraped and the bowl and cup were pushed in. It was the same dreary, foul-tasting slush but he ate it fast, drank the plain water – after first tasting it; if there had been even the faintest hint of saltiness, he wouldn't touch it. But this time it was OK.

It must be the night-time meal, which meant they wouldn't collect the empty bowl and cup until daylight – or maybe not until they brought him another meal, which could be another twenty-four hours – or any time in between.

He had to use what time he had – and use it well.

The nail point slipped under one edge of one of the stones but the metal began to bend with the upward pressure he put on it, without budging the flagstone. Sweating, panting, he sat back on his hams, wondering how he was going to lift the stone.

His fingertips told him he had tried to move the biggest stone; the other one, closest to the wall, was only half the size. So he pushed his nail under one edge and tried again. At first nothing happened, except he tore a fingernail and cursed at the pain. Using his uninjured hand, he managed to lift the stone a half-inch: enough space to slip his fingers under. He froze when the stone made a hollow, scraping noise as it slid out of its bedding and across the one next to it. His own panting and the blood rushing in his ears killed any possibility of hearing any one opening the door flap, so he gritted his teeth, lifted the stone aside and then took out the larger flagstone, setting it down as carefully as he could. A shallow hole was revealed.

Leaning into the hole, which smelled of moist earth, he groped around the side nearest the door and after what seemed like a half an hour – it was barely two minutes – he touched the protruding end of the small tin Mulvaney had mentioned.

The nail point prised open the lid of the rust-scabbed metal box. It hadn't eaten into the tin very much yet and he felt the wadded map and, underneath the paper, several wax-stemmed, strike-anywhere vestas. He counted them, ten in all.

He took one between his teeth, climbed out of the hole, and groped for his blanket. He moved the wooden bowl and tin cup away from the flap and spread the blanket across the bottom of the door. This would prevent a line of light showing under the door when he struck the match. Meantime, he had to hope no one would come to collect the dishes.

Caine reared back and clamped his eyes closed hurriedly as the match flared: even this short time in total darkness had made them ultra-sensitive.

Squinting, opening his eyelids gradually, he was able to see well enough. Damn! The end of that removable brick showed too clearly, would be spotted almost immediately by anyone with a lantern. What could he fill in the gap with. . . ?

It was obvious: it had to be some of the 'mortar' he had dug out from around the flagstones. Then, of course, there wouldn't be enough to put back around the flagstones.

'OK!' he said in a loud whisper which had him cringing as the single word seemed to echo around the walls. 'To hell with the brick. What's it matter if they see it? By then the cell'll be empty and all they'll be interested in is where I've gone – but, to play it safe, it means I'll have to go – now!'

His belly tightened at the thought. He had intended to investigate the shaft, its size and depth, then plan his descent in accordance with what he found. If he could pull the flagstones back into place after getting into the shaft, they might not be noticed right off when the guards discovered the empty cell – the guards would spend a little time discussing the shaft. Not much. Only minutes. But that briefest of delays could be important to Caine.

Mulvaney had said to dig through the bottom of the

pit under the flagstones – *Only a couple of feet.* But what did he dig with? The bowl and the tin cup. At that stage it wouldn't matter if they were missing when someone came to collect them. The fact that he was missing would be their main concern.

He had no idea how long it took him to remove that two feet of packed earth but it took a lot of sweat and aching muscles. The air seemed thicker and he was breathing raggedly as he piled the dirt around the hole on the floor; so much for his original idea of hiding his exit!

One leg suddenly plunged through the last few inches and in a surge of panic he grabbed at the flagstones on the edge of the hole. He could feel cool, almost cold air around his leg and then, tightening his grip, he kicked more of the earth away, heard it scattering and falling down the shaft. There was a kind of low, surging sound below, not quite a muted roar but definitely the sound of the water flowing down there.

How far down? No way of telling. He climbed out, sat on the edge of the hole, kicked away all of the remaining fringe of dirt. As it fell he fumbled out one more wax vesta, struck it across the flagstone beside him, let it flare and burn well, then dropped it into the shaft.

It was very lightweight, fluttered from side to side, briefly lighting up dirt walls. But it was extinguished long before it reached the bottom. He rolled back, grabbed his blanket and tore off a strip of the thin material. He used one more vesta to light it and as it flared, let it drop, having knotted a small stone from the shaft wall into the base. He strained to see below. There was a glint of something down there, blurred; probably the reflection of the burning rag in the moving water, and then blackness again.

Caine gulped. It might only be ten feet, but to him it appeared as if the shaft descended into the bowels of the earth.

But there could be no turning back now.

If he backed out and stayed, and his escape attempt was discovered – as it would be – what he had thought was a taste of hell so far would be a Sunday school picnic compared to what they would do to him.

It took a deal of courage to descend into that narrow shaft. His shoulders touched the walls. His toes felt as if they were breaking off as they took his full weight, his fingers digging in desperately. He had torn more strips off the blanket – to hell with any light that might escape under the door. He'd wrapped them around his hands and feet and knees, using the whole of the blanket. By bringing his entire body into use, pressing with feet, knees, backside, shoulders and hands against the walls, he descended slowly. Clods of earth broke away and fell into the blackness. He couldn't be sure whether he heard them splashing into the water or not.

He would find out soon enough.

More quickly than he intended! He lost a grip with one knee, and it was too late for the foot that was dangling in mid-air to take the strain, although he drove his aching toes hard into the earthen wall. But the dirt crumbled and then he was falling – falling. Flesh was scraped from his shoulders and elbows and upper arms.

His legs were grazed, his buttocks, too. His head banged against the wall several times. Crumbling dirt filled his hair, ears, nostrils and mouth, somehow forcing its way in. His eyes were squeezed shut to save them from the grit and. . . .

He thought he had slammed into rock, he struck so hard. But his body plunged down into the water and he just had time enough to suck down a decent breath before he was totally submerged.

He was completely disoriented, his body flung upside down, whirled around, bouncing off rock walls that had, fortunately, been worn smooth over many years by millions of gallons of water flowing through the subterranean tunnel.

But where was it taking him? How far did it go? *Where the hell was the surface?* If he didn't get another breath in a matter of seconds it wouldn't matter where the surface was!

His feet touched bottom – he hoped it was bottom and not the roof. He had been spun so many times he couldn't be sure which way was up. He let his legs bend and then he snapped them straight as fast and as hard as he could, putting one hand above his head in case he crashed his skull.

His hand touched the smooth rock – it was sliding past at a good rate. He still didn't know whether he was right way up, kept his hand against the rock, feeling it whip by. Bright lights were whirling behind his eyes. He was choking. His chest was being crushed, so was his belly, forcing his insides up into his throat—

He was dying.

77

Then his hand felt different. *Yes!* Yes, his fingers were wiggling *in air!* His instincts had taken over before the thoughts had been processed by his brain. He threw his head back and his face burst through. Still no light, of course; the sensation of rushing was very strong – water gurgled into his mouth. He snapped it closed quickly, breathed in through his nose an instant before water fully encased his head again.

Then he realized that the tunnel was narrowing.

His shoulders were touching more often now. He had to draw his legs up a little, quickly let them float out behind his body so that he was horizontal. His hands could touch the walls sliding past on any side he reached for. The flow was increasing in pace – confirming that the tunnel was narrowing down into what could be the equivalent of a water pipe: maybe too narrow for his body to pass through. He would be jammed tight, the relentless pressure of the water pulping him until the flesh ripped away and allowed what was left to break apart and spew out of the the end of the tunnel. . . .

God! What a way to die! So – senseless – so. . . .

He started to spin and was unable to stop the movement. The last few bubbles of breath were squeezed out of his mouth and his brain began to shut down without oxygen.

Then he was shot out into the cool, star-studded night like a ball from a cannon's mouth.

He gagged, trying to snatch a breath as he felt himself tumbling. He plunged into water again, going deep in a roar of bubbles around his head. His eyes felt as if they were turning inside out. Water surged up his notrils and down his throat, his hands clawed wildly – first at water, then at – nothing.

Nothing but fresh air.

He didn't remember dragging himself up on to solid ground. It felt strange when he came round slowly, his head feeling as if it had been split by a tomahawk. It felt even worse when he sat up, his fingers digging into grass and coarse sand, fireworks exploding behind his eyes.

It was coming on to daybreak; the sky, peach-coloured in the east, was shot through with widening rays of the sun. Deep shadows surrounded him and he shaded his eyes as he looked up at towering walls studded with rocks and brush. He was on the edge of a deep pool; water surged out of the wall in front of him, some ten or twelve feet up, hitting a slope of boulders where it turned to spray and trickled before reaching the pool.

He must have been flung out of that hole by the rushing water. Thank God it had had enough power to hurl him beyond those rocks.

He had never been here, but he realized this was the fishpond that some of the inmates had spoken of. If a prisoner was well-behaved, for a long time, he was sometimes rewarded with kitchen duties, part of which was to catch fish for the warden's supper. It was a desired position, not simply because it was easy, but because a man could get some decent food inside him, and one man had said there were two wooden boats they used to fish in the deepest waters.

It had been a fantasy, of course, thinking someone might be able to use one of those boats to get away – not with armed guards watching from the bank.

But Caine didn't have any guards and, though his whole body hurt and ached and throbbed, he started searching. It was full daylight before he found the boats and a small jetty almost hidden by reeds. There were two dinghies, clinker-built, both with a few inches of water sloshing about the bottoms. Poles and oars lay on the bank amongst the grass.

Caine sat down and looked at the deep pool. It seemed placid enough but there were underwater swirls and he saw where the outlet was, joining the main creek and flowing downstream. One of those boats could drift at a good rate in that current, be carried quite a way from here before the discovery of Mulvaney and his own escape. No, better just think of it as his absence right now.

There was a long way to go. Downstream would take him back towards town where maybe he could steal some clothes and food, even a gun. They would expect that, anyway, and concentrate the search there, but there seemed no way around it. . . .

Unless. . . .

Over the next hour, his nerves on the edge of screaming in case his absence had already been discovered, expecting a shot from an armed searcher any second, he carried some rocks to one of the dinghies and placed them in the bottom. Using reeds, he lashed one oar over the transom, like an angled rudder, climbed into the other boat and rowed out into the middle of the pool, towing the laden one, again using knotted reeds to make the tow-line.

It broke but it didn't matter – it snapped just near the outlet of the pool, where the narrowing of the banks increased the current's rate. He untied the boat with the rocks in the bottom, guided it through and let it go in midstream.

The current snatched it away from him, the trailing oar blade biting in and keeping it on a more or less straight course as it sped downstream. How far it would go before the reeds broke and the oar dropped off, so that the boat would probably nose in towards the bank and catch in some reeds or underwater snags, he didn't know. They might wonder about the layer of rocks, but often river fishermen used this method of giving their boat more stability so they could better control it in a strong current. He left a strip of his jail blanket caught under a couple of the rocks . . . that ought to help keep them searching this area for quite some time.

They would expect that he would drift downstream in one of the boats, so when they found what they expected, the search would be concentrated down here – while he rowed the second boat away, *upstream*, putting a lot of distance between himself and the hunters.

It was all he could think of right now; he was tired and wanted to sleep, but there was no time for that.

He had taken the only way out of the Big Pen, and now he had to keep going. If he gave in to tiredness they would soon catch him and drag him back.

And that would be the end: he would be there for the rest of his life. Which might not be very long once they got their hands on him again.

CHAPTER 7

FREEDOM?

Rowing the boat against the current was going to kill him. That was his reluctant conclusion after his arms felt as if they were falling off, his neck muscles screamed with fiery pain, and his shoulders knotted, bringing tightness and breathlessness.

He rested on the oars and immediately felt the old dinghy start to move backwards. What puzzled him was that the current didn't appear all that strong. He could trail his fingers overside and the pressure against them was enough to cause ripples, but only small ones.

He couldn't rest for long or he would lose much of the distance he had gained. Looking back, he could still see the strange cascade of water where he had emerged from the underground tunnel. *Half a mile!* Not far enough.

Caine angled the boat in towards the reeds growing out from the bank and rammed the nose into them with a couple of energetic thrusts of the oars. They held the boat, which would give him a little time to take another look at his situation; it was nowhere near as good as he wanted.

It was pleasant, though, to scoop up handfuls of water and let it trickle down his burning throat – and not have to worry about his bowels being knotted up by Epsom Salts. That was one plus! What else did he have?

He was free – or, at least outside the walls of that damn hell-hole. Above the rim of the cliffs he could see part of the prison, dark, grey and brooding like some of those old English castles he had seen illustrated in books. There were guards on the walls, as in those old days, but they carried weapons more deadly than longbows or pikes or battle axes. . . .

Still, the inmates claimed a job as wall guard was in big demand with the prison staff: no one expected anyone to break out so a man could relax up there, pick a shady spot in summer, a warm corner out of the wind in winter.

But he couldn't feel too complacent; there was sure to be some eager beaver who would be watching with sharp eyes, looking to ingratiate himself with the warden. If he could see the prison walls, someone up there would have at least a partial view of this river – why it was called a creek he didn't know. It was wide enough and deep enough to qualify as a river.

What the hell was he doing? Letting his mind wander when he had to concentrate, focus on his escape.

He was wearing only the ragged trousers of the prison uniform. The shirt had been torn to shreds by his descent down the shaft. His skin was raw on his shoulders and knuckles and legs, despite wrapping strips of blanket around places he had figured as being vulnerable to damage by the rough earthen walls.

The sun was already burning the white, though begrimed, skin of his back. He could feel his skull warming up too, despite his thick crown of dark, wet hair. His feet were cut and bare. He needed clothes, especially boots. He also needed decent food, and a gun – and, probably most of all, a horse.

He had to put as much distance between himself and the prison as he could, and find a farm or small ranch. . . .

For all he knew, they might have already spotted the other dinghy drifting downstream, or, if it had already nosed into the bank, they could be organizing pursuit. They would search upstream as well as down, though downstream would get priority – he hoped. *Easy now: don't panic. . . . It's too soon for searches.* It wasn't likely that Mulvaney's body had been found yet. As it happened, it wouldn't be discovered until after midnight, so he had a good start even though he was unaware of it.

The restless years after the war, when he and Ray got into all kinds of scrapes, had taught him something about being a fugitive. He would be in great danger once the escape was known and a posse had been formed. The members would be relentless, and the warden might even give an order to shoot on sight; he wouldn't want it known that anyone had managed to break out, whether subsequently the escape attempt

85

was successful or not.

Caine had been in greater danger a hundred times during the war, of course, but eventually that had become a way of life; his instincts were honed razor-sharp, ready for instant reaction.

Those instincts had been somewhat blunted with the years that had since passed and now he had nowhere to run.

Just – *run. Stay free.* He might or might not link up with Ray Porteus again, but even if he did, could he rely on Ray to help him? Sure – until he found out what Caine knew about Mulvaney's gold.

Then it would be anybody's guess what happened after that.

OK, he was on the run, alone. It would be best not to count on any outside help. So get the hell moving, get away from here into different country, then review the situation and alter plans according to events.

He waded ashore, found some big rocks and smashed them through the bottom of the boat. He could make better progress ashore, instead of breaking his back fighting that current. It might be more dangerous, but he could widen the gap between himself and the Big Pen with more speed on land.

He pulled up armfuls of reeds, draped them over the side of the boat to disguise its outline, submerged the oars and anchored them on the creek bottom with more rocks.

Then he continued on upstream, wading knee-to-waist-deep, staying in close to the bank, pulling himself along by reeds or the branches of scrubby bushes growing close enough for him to reach. There were insects and bugs galore but he just dunked his head, even his whole body, when they became too pesky. Once a deadly water moccasin wriggled past him, not a hand's breadth from his belly, and he felt his bowels quiver. But the snake kept going, likely as startled as he was.

Still, he climbed out, found himself a hefty stick and took it with him when he lowered himself down into the water again.

The glare hurt his eyes. His belly growled, sloshing with all the water he had kept drinking in an effort to assuage his raging thirst. Under the overhang of a weeping willow a few yards from the water's edge, he found shade and a small patch of wild onions. Not his favourite food, but he crunched and munched at the juicy stalks and bulbs, had to gulp even more water to ease the burning in his mouth.

Fatigue and the long weeks of tension and bad food were catching up with him. It was quiet here under the willow, well hidden, but a search party would check out such places as a matter of course. He had better move on. He started to struggle up, then fell back with a sigh. *Too tired.*

He felt himself sliding down into sleep, tried to fight it, but his body knew that it needed recuperative rest. In minutes, despite himself, he was curled up like a cat, in a deep sleep.

Mulvaney's body was not discovered until twenty-four hours after he died.

The evening pigswill was pushed through the doorflap with a cup of water and two tablets, supposedly to treat Mull's ailing heart, but they were only plain lactose instead of digitalis. 'Doc' Russell figured to make Mulvaney tell him where he had stashed the gold bars in exchange for the genuine medicine. The guards changed shifts at midnight and the relieved man was supposed to collect the empty food utensils, but the man who reached into Mulvaney's cell cursed as cold grey oatmeal in the wooden bowl slopped over his hand.

'Goddammit! You old bastard! Whyn't you eat your grub!' He hammered on the door with his fist and kicked it, just to make a racket and interrupt Mulvaney's sleep. There was no response, of course. The guard, murmuring, knelt by the flap again and groped for the tin cup of water. This splashed on his hand, too, and he bit off another curse. At least it washed some of the sticky oatmeal off. But it should have been empty! All prisoners complained there was never enough to drink. Cups were *always* empty upon collection. With an uncomfortable hunch now scratching at the back of his brain, the guard felt around and – *yes, dammit!* He found the untouched so-called heart tablets.

In seconds he had the door open and had drawn the cover back on the bullseye lantern, directing the spot of light around the walls of the cell – on to the dead man lying there.

'Goddammit to hell!'

When he opened the door of Caine's cell, the guard

felt his legs turn to rubber and a deep sickness in his belly as he saw the flagstones half-buried beneath the pile of dirt scooped from the gaping shaft – and, of course, no sign of the man he knew as Frank Keller.

The warden raised hell at being awakened, but when he was told the news: one of the oldest prisoners dead, another gone through a hole in the floor, he almost had a fit.

Every cell in solitary was opened up and the bewildered inmates dragged out, questioned, and when, naturally, they claimed they had heard or seen nothing, they were beaten just for the hell of it before being thrown back into their stone coffins.

Word was sent to town and Sheriff Gaskell was no happier than the warden at being dragged out of his warm bed to be ordered to get together a posse of at least ten men.

'Hell almighty! It's the middle of the goddamn night!'

'Well, pardon me, Sheriff,' said Killane, the deputy warden, sarcastically, 'but our prisoners seem to prefer night-time for escapin' rather than in daylight! Now, get those men mounted and fitted out. Make damn sure they have guns and plenty of ammunition. This is a dead-or-alive manhunt – preferably dead.'

But there really was little that could be done in the dark and Killane had to fume and rage until the first grey of daylight vaguely outlined the hills.

Then the two posses, one from the jail, the other from town, spread out, searching all the way from the prison and along the banks of the creek. It wasn't long before the grounded dinghy was discovered and Sheriff Gaskell growled at his men to spread out both sides of the creek and head downstream.

Killane watched, belly churning, knowing the filthy mood the warden would be in when given the news. Then a man from the sheriff's posse rode up.

'Warden, Sher'ff says you might like to send some men to search upstream, too.'

Killane glared. 'He did, huh? And why the hell would he think I'd *like* to do that when the damn boat this Keller used is found headin' *down*stream?'

The townsman wasn't fazed by Killane's anger. 'Says this might've been a decoy – some reeds've been found in the bottom of the boat that look like they could've held an oar in place over the transom – like a rudder.'

Killane frowned. 'I've seen that done. Makes it easier to steer.'

'Sheriff thinks them rocks in the bottom might've been to give it weight, so it could drift down this way on the current, empty, while Keller headed t'other way, upstream.'

Goddamn! It was possible! And Killane would have to make sure the warden knew that his deputy had thought of this possibility – and had acted upon it.

'All right. Six men, that group at the edge of the trees. Start ridin' upstream, fast! Just in case Keller's tryin' to hornswoggle us with this here boat caught in the reeds! Let it drift down while he went t'other way.'

There! Now eveyone had heard him give the order to make the other search upstream. Christ! He hoped they found some sign of Keller before dark or he might end up in solitary.

He felt better when the six men spurred their mounts away, heading upstream. No matter which way he had gone, Frank Keller wouldn't get far before he was recaptured.

Then God help the poor bastard!

But Caine had made the most of his head start.

He could hardly believe his luck as the hours passed and there were no signs of pursuit. Any posse that had been formed must still be occupied downstream, he hoped the dinghy had managed to get a long way before the current finally grounded it.

He had had some more good luck, too, which was always encouraging to a man on the run. He tended to be a mite superstitious and good omens always gave him a boost.

Such as awakening after his sleep under the willow to find, or rather, hear a horse cropping grass only a few yards outside the line of creekbank timber. It was saddleless, but there were broken hobble ropes dangling from its left foreleg. Must have busted loose during the night and wandered off – which could mean someone would be coming looking for the animal.

He took a chance; stood just within the shadow of the timber where the horse could see him, and whistled softly. The animal, chomping some of the lush grass, lifted its head indolently and looked towards him. It didn't spook when, after a cautious look around, Caine stepped out, talking gently as he approached the horse, a blue-grey mare, several years old. He could see marks from harness straps worn into the chest and withers, and figured it likely had been used to pull a plough; there were farms around this area, though he couldn't see any from here in the gathering dusk.

The mare backed off a few times before it would allow him to stroke its muzzle and rub behind its ears. It nuzzled him, well used to people, and in a few minutes he was astride its back, using the mane and his skinned knees to guide the animal away from the creek, heading north.

It was just on dark when he saw the farm building and the glow of a cigarette in the dark doorway; the farmer was likely looking out for the return of his horse.

Caine dismounted behind some trees, patted the mare once more, then slapped it across the rump. It snorted and trotted forward, turning after a few yards towards the house.

The farmer, a solid-built man, stepped out of the doorway, flicking the cigarette away, and whistled through his teeth. The mare moved towards him. Caine watched as the man gave it an affectionate rub between the ears and led the animal into a small corral, where two more horses stood, curious, but unmoving. The farmer went into the barn and came out with a nosebag, likely oats. Caine smiled slightly; the man at least seemed like a human being. He had been wondering just how the farmer would treat a horse that had busted its hobbles and wandered off for an unknown time.

So he felt kind of bad about getting down on his

belly and writhing into the corn patch, reaching up to snap off three ripening cobs. He sat there among the stalks, in the fading light, tearing off the leaves and biting into the juicy kernels.

He had almost finished the third cob when the stalks in front of him parted slowly and a shotgun muzzle seemed to grow out of the leaves, stopping a few inches from his face.

'That's my corn, mister!'

'It is – and I've stole three cobs. And I don't have no money to pay for 'em.'

Caine's ready admission seemed to puzzle the farmer. Then the gun jerked towards the low house, where a dim light burned, outlining the doorway now as the stars appeared one by one. 'Your legs left their sweat marks on my mare. Knew someone'd been ridin' her and they'd treated her well enough. I'm guessin' you've upset the warden of the Big Pen by escapin'. That close?'

'I'll . . . just push on, if it's OK by you, friend. I don't want any trouble.'

'Bet you don't! But you'll find plenty if you're on the dodge.'

The man waited, as if for some explanation, but Caine didn't offer any.

'If you're runnin' from that hell-hole and can still treat a runaway mare well, I figure you're someone worth gettin' to know.'

Caine frowned. 'Mister, I'm in no position to be socializing. If you've got an old set of overalls I could have, and mebbe some boots, I'll be on my way. I give

93

you my word I'll pay you soon as I'm able and. . . .'

He stopped because the farmer was laughing. 'By Godfrey, I got me a real-life comedian here! Take the word of an escaped convict? Hey, feller, I used to drive the pick-up wagon for the Big Pen before I got married – and I never seen a single one of them convicts I took to the jail I'd trust enough to polish my boots. They'd likely put 'em on an' run off.'

'Don't blame you. But I mean it. I will pay you for any help you give me. It might take a little time, but you'll get whatever you ask.'

'How about five hundred bucks?' the man said quickly.

Caine was stunned. 'Well, if that's your figure – and you won't come down – it'll be a real long time before I can get that much together. But I'll do it if I have to.'

'Forget it! Come on up to the house and I'll feed you a beefsteak and potatoes, if your belly'll take it after prison chow. I'll see what I can find in the way of clothin'. Had a tall streak of misery workin' for me some time back and I think he left some trousers and a shirt. Well, come on! Don't look like you just sat on a hot poker. I'm offerin' help. You want it or not?'

'I want it. I *need* it. Can't help but wonder why you're doing it.'

The farmer paused, looking directly at Caine, scalp to toenails. 'Mister, I'm mostly a law-abidin' man, been that way all my life. I'm a widower without children and all I want is to be left in peace and work my farm. But . . . last winter I seen a fella in my cornpatch, just like you, walkin' scarecrow. Had to've been from the Big

94

Pen. Was decidin' whether to go help him when a posse showed up. He run, staggerin' like he was taperin' off from a week-old drunk, he was so tuckered out. They rode him down, beat him to bloody pulp, then shot him. Big feller, Killane I think he called hisself, rode up with two men. Told me I never seen nothin'. That man they killed was a wanted outlaw on the run. If I ever thought different and spoke up about what I'd seen, they'd burn my farmhouse – with me in it.'

Caine was silent for a few moments, then nodded his head. 'I'll leave as soon as I get some clothes – and I won't forget your money.'

'Hell, I was joshin' about that. Send me a card lettin' me know you made it. That'll do me. Now come on. Let's make the most of the dark hours.'

CHAPTER 8

TRAIL TO NOWHERE

Russ Campion looked a little more prepossessing than he had at the end of the war, in his rags of Confederate uniform, long hair, beetling brows and pugnacious jaw and all.

He looked a little better, but that face would still scare a sick child half to death. The eyebrows were kept trimmed down to bushy, the hair, while long at the sides and back of his neck, was manageable and clean enough. The jaw still stuck out like a frigate's bow cleaving the waves, under a thin line of moustache, and the pale-blue eyes were stark against the leather-coloured skin. A few streaks of grey showed in that hair, but the man moved lithely: fit for his age and profession.

His pin-striped trousers and the vest buttoned over a

pale-blue shirt had all seen better days but fitted him well. He looked at Killane bleakly. 'You're wasting too much damn time down here, you fool!'

'Who're you talkin' to, sawbones?' Killane bristled. 'You ain't even s'posed to be here!'

'I have an interest in the escaped prisoner.'

'Hell, we don't have no escaped prisoner. Man on the run, sure, but he'll be dragged back and soon brought down to the common denominator once we get him back to solitary.'

'You won't find him down here. I was with him for months at the end of the war. He wasn't much more'n a shaver then. But he was smart, earned the two chevrons they gave him – used his brains. Saved the whole troop's hides one time, got a medal for it. He can easy outfox the likes of you and Gaskell, Killane.'

'Seems to me you're oversteppin' the mark, Doc. You ain't even officially on the penitentiary payroll.'

'That's true. I'm just a civic-minded sawbones, trying to help the unfortunate men in your care in that damn hell-hole.'

Killane sneered. 'Known you for quite a spell, sawbones. You never done nothin' you didn't figure would make you a profit somehow. Be good to know your interest in Mulvaney – an' now this man Keller, who was pract'ly his cell-mate.'

'Doc' Russell smiled crookedly. 'For one thing, his name's Caine not Keller. Got you with that one, huh? Yeah, Caine's a mighty interestin' character.' He looked at his right hand with a knotted scar about the size of a dollar on the back. He moved the fingers stiffly. Mouth tight, he said, 'I'll bet you your month's pay against a stack of gold bars you won't find him down here. He's gone upstream – and I'm heading that way. Mebbe you'd like to come along?'

Killane frowned: the sawbones was moving too fast for him. 'I've got my job to do, but what's this about gold bars?'

'Figured that might get your attention. You're the kind of man I need to back me in this, Killane. Forget that stupid sheriff. Let him work his posse all over down here; they won't find what they're looking for. You ride upstream with me and maybe I'll tell you a story about them six gold bars.'

Killane's frown deepened. 'You want me to quit?'

Russell Campion shrugged. 'Up to you. Gold bars are worth a lot more'n this piddling job'll ever pay you.'

'You know where you can find six gold bars?' the deputy warden asked carefully.

'No. But I think Caine does.'

'You mean Keller? You only *think* he knows?'

'He wouldn't run if he didn't. They found a loose brick between his cell and Mulvaney's – and Mulvaney's the one who stashed the gold. Him and Caine always got along pretty good.'

Killane spat. 'Sounds kind of. . . .' He held out his hand flat, and waggled it from side to side.

Campion sighed and nodded. 'Yeah, it does. But I'm strong on hunches, always have been. I've chased this gold for ten years. Red Stevens was part of it but he's out for keeps now. You look like a man who'd take a gamble, Killane. Now time's a'wasting; you gonna join me and grow rich, or stay loyal to that loco warden and grow old and poor in that stinkin' pen?'

After a brief silence, Killane said, 'Just the two of us?'

'Well, if you know a couple or three men you can trust. . . . Only thing is, it cuts down your share.'

'My share! What about yours?'

'I'm the one providing the gold in the first place. I take half. The rest is yours – or whosever you want to divvy-up with.'

Killane smiled thinly. 'Glad I was never sick enough to have to see you for treatment, *Doc*!'

Campion smiled crookedly. 'That's the deal.'

'Uh-huh. That's OK. I know a couple men would come in mighty handy – in fact, both are with the posses. And I'll see them right when it comes time to share out them gold bars.'

Russ Campion nodded. 'Bet you will, being the kind of fair-minded *hombre* you are. There's an Indian with Gaskell, the one with the unpronounceable name. He's a good tracker. They've used him before.'

'We just call him Paco. But Gaskell won't part with him.'

'Steal him then. We need him. Promise him whatever he wants.'

Killane nodded, smiling thinly. 'You done a lot more'n doctorin' in your time, sawbones.'

'I'm versatile,' Campion admitted. 'OK, we've wasted enough time. Get your men and let's get on Caine's real trail.'

Caine was a long way ahead of any of the posses, even

the one that had travelled upstream on the off-chance that he might have gone that way.

When he had left they hadn't discovered the sunken dinghy, but they were scouring the area thoroughly, working their way towards MacAdam's farm.

The farmer had provided Caine with clothing, old and wrinkled but tolerably clean and in fair condition; about what a drifter would be expected to wear. The boots were a little run-over at the heels and a shade tighter than Caine liked, but he wasn't about to look a gift horse in the mouth. He had a buff-coloured hat with a hole in the peak worn through from being pinched between finger and thumb when putting on and removing the hat. He even had a sun-faded neckerchief, some grub in sagging saddle-bags and a half-broke horse.

MacAdam had said, 'You might've seen three horses in my corral. They're my work team – and they wear my brand.'

Caine had nodded. 'Sure. If they run me down they'll trace the horse to you and you'll be in more trouble than. . . .'

'But . . . I ran down a mustang, a mare, couple weeks back. Done some work on her but she's only half-broke. Pretty good nature, and I reckon she'll stand for a man on her back. Best of all, no brand – and the saddle gear I'll give you is old stuff, untraceable.'

'If I find those gold bars I told you about, I'd better give you one to square away all this.'

MacAdam shook his head. 'No. After I seen what Killane and his crew done to the other ranny who'd tried to escape, I swore to myself if any fugitive come through here, I wouldn't turn him over to that crew of butchers.'

'Still, I won't forget your help, Mac.'

They shook hands and Caine rode out after dark. The black mare acted up a little, but seemed good-natured as Mac had said.

The one thing he wished he did have was a gun. But the farmer only had his shotgun and a cap-and-ball Navy Colt by way of firearms. The Colt had been given to him on his tenth wedding anniversary by his late wife and he couldn't bring himself to part with it.

Caine savvied that, but he felt uncomfortable, knowing men were hunting him and he was unarmed.

Mac had drawn him a rough map, showing how best to get across this country and down into a pass that would take him to Dragoon County. It seemed the best way to go.

Caine had opened the rusted tin again and carefully folded out the paper on which Mulvaney had drawn his map in charcoal, not having a proper pencil or pen and ink. The lines had been heavy but had smeared during their tight folding and the long sojourn in the buried tin.

Names of places and landmarks were hard to make out. There was one advantage: Caine recalled Red Stevens saying that the night Mull had slipped away with the mule, and presumably the gold bars, they had been camped in an area of hills and canyons called the Jackhammers, named after an unsuccessful attempt to cut a pass through the foothills to allow a nearby

101

railroad to run out a spur track. Bad weather and a flood which, locals said, reoccurred at random intervals put an end to the project.

Red had backtracked Mulvaney a little way before being forced to abort as Yankee patrols were in the area.

'Far as I could figure, he'd gone south of our camp. How far south is anyone's guess. But there're mountains down that way where a man could easy hide six bars of gold.'

When they had a chance Caine and Ray Porteus had looked up a survey map. The nearest hills named had been the Sawbacks, but there had been no time to check further.

Taking the trail that MacAdam recommended would eventually get him down to these rugged hills. But whether they were the ones Mulvaney had stashed the gold in, no one knew.

The charcoal had smeared too much, obliterating features and names. But there weren't many. A lump of charcoal was not an ideal tool for drawing a detailed map. Enough of a couple of letters showed that *seemed* to fit or make up part of the names they knew from the survey map: what could be a 'wb' followed after a short space by a hook that might be part of an 'S' and so part of the word Sawbacks.

But it was mighty chancy. None of the other partly legible letters could give Caine any more confidence that he was on the right trail.

There was one thing the farmer had said that kept Caine heading in that direction though, with a smidgen of hope. . . .

Mac had said, 'You'll have plenty of cover in those hills, anyway. And if you keep on, you'll come to Dragoon County. The only law there is when the sheriff from Bayliss rides across – about three times a year, just to let folks know he's still around and will be standing for re-election.'

Dragoon County. Could Mull, with his pain-slurred speech and speaking through the small brick hole in the thick wall, have said 'Dragoon' and not 'dragon', as Caine had thought?

It might only be a coincidence, but Caine had little else to go on, so had nothing to lose by checking it out.

If he could make that far.

The six men originally sent upstream by Killane, at Gaskell's suggestion had found nothing of interest. They were riding around aimlessly, supposedly searching for tracks, when Campion and Killane arrived with the Indian and the two hardcases, Tex Arlin and Hashknife O'Hare.

Killane sent the six men back to Gaskell and while he was doing this the Indian 'breed, Paco, rode in to MacAdam's farm. He was met by the farmer with his shotgun.

'You're off your reservation, chief. This is private land.'

Paco said nothing, kneed his half-wild pony across to where MacAdam had been burning some trash. The 'breed, despite vocal protests from the farmer, dismounted, hunkered down and poked at the ashes with his hunting knife.

'Listen. You savvy American, chief? Watch my mouth: git back on your bronc and git off my land.' MacAdam cocked the shotgun, turned quickly as he heard riders approaching. 'What the hell? My day for visitors.'

He felt a tightening of his belly as he recognized Killane.

The deputy warden looked past him. 'Got somethin' interestin, Paco?'

The 'breed held up a piece of charred, rotting grey cloth on the end of his knife blade. Killane shook his head slowly, looking down at MacAdam.

'Bear Creek Grey. Special fashion for our prisoners, chose by the warden hiself. You seem to be in a deal of trouble, sodbuster.'

'I ain't the one covered by a cocked shotgun!'

The deputy warden widened his smirk, spoke to one of the hardcases.

'You gonna do somethin' about that and earn your keep, Tex? Or, if you feel so inclined Hashknife, you can help out. . . .'

MacAdam didn't know which way to look as they put space between their mounts, moving sideways. While he was watching the one called Tex, Hashknife drew his six-gun in a blurring movement and triggered. The farmer started to spin but the bullet took him in the upper leg, which folded under him, like the blade of a claspknife closing. Before he hit the ground Tex had put two bullets into him, flinging his solid body face down in the dirt. The shotgun clattered but did not fire.

'Goddamn idiots!' roared Doc Russell Campion. 'We

104

wanted him alive!'

'He's still breathin', sawbones,' Killane said as MacAdam rolled on to one side, coughing and gasping, his chest and lower ribs all bloody. Killane folded his hands on the saddle horn and leaned forward, smiling coldly down at the wounded farmer. 'Bad luck for you, MacAdam. Paco, bring your knife over here. . . .'

Caine had been on the run for three days now.

The mare was holding up but was cantankerous at unexpected moments. He was worried that it might choose such a moment to remind him of who was really boss here when trackers were within sight, or that he would have difficulty in covering the mare's rebellious sign where its hoofs had churned the ground.

He had paused on the crest of one of the ranges he was crossing, dismounted and tethered the horse securely, while he parted the bushes just enough to see the country he had recently passed over.

No riders. So far, so good.

He continued on, occasionally deliberately leaving tracks going more to the north. It wouldn't throw a good tracker for long, but any delay was acceptable right now. MacAdam's map was helpful, more detailed than he had hoped.

But he sure wished he had a gun.

By noon of the fourth day he was travelling within sight of the distant badlands. This was the far side of the alkali from that where he and Ray had found Red Stevens. But he swore bitterly; he had come way too far north. He should be skirting the badlands so far to the south that he couldn't even see them. But now there was that familiar milky haze as the desert winds whirled and spun and gusted, throwing particles of alkali into the air.

He stopped by a waterhole he came upon unexpectedly, filled his leaky canteen – the only one MacAdam had had to spare – and prised some gum off the rough bark of a tree, using it to try and at least partly stop the leak.

He kicked his heels into the mare's flanks when he was mounted, impatient to be away from this area. The horse didn't care for the kick, swerved against the pull of the bit and whipped her head around, trying to bite his leg. This went on for almost a hundred yards until eventually she ran him into heavy brush. Trying to fight the animal's great strength was a losing battle and he crashed into the brush. She convulsed and scraped him off against a tree. Or rather, to save a broken leg, he threw it over the saddle horn and jumped clear, ending awkwardly caught up in the bushes while the mare ran off.

He got to his feet as fast as he could, whistled, called, but he could hear the horse running on and making its own path through the shoulder-high bushes.

Well, it would be easy to track but it might not stop for miles now it had made its bid for freedom. It could easily get rid of the saddle rig by rubbing against boulders or trees; the old leather was close to rotten and wouldn't hold up for long with such treatment.

'Nice work, Josh. Now you're afoot, nowhere near where you wanted to go, no water or grub or weapons, except the worn old hunting knife. Might as well find a shady spot near the waterhole and have a sleep while I'm waiting for them to find me!' He kicked at a low bush in self-anger.

He sighed, brushed himself down and started following the broken path the mare had made through the bushes. If he didn't come up with her again before dark he would be finished.

What it meant was that he would be as good as dead when they caught up with him, as they would do, and maybe it would be not too long before it happened.

He cut a sapling about five feet long, sat on a boulder and hacked a point on one end. He filled his pockets with egg-sized stones, pulled a handful of dry brush and held it with the stick, making sure he could reach his vestas in his short pocket in a hurry.

None of these improvised weapons offered more than mild comfort; OK in a hand-to-hand fight, but a man with a gun would simply shoot him from beyond the reach of the stones or the crude spear.

But it was all he could do right now. He could no longer hear the horse smashing a path through the brush. It might mean the mare had stopped, or had simply broken away into more open country.

He pushed on.

By sundown Caine hadn't found the mare. Once he smelled and later found fresh dung, and followed the tracks off to one side. They led him out of the brush area on to a slope of scattered trees.

There was movement down below, halfway, but he wasn't sure what it was; there were too many shadows

107

and too many animals returned to their lairs or chosen sleeping places at this time. He tightened his grip on the spear. There were bound to be big cats in these mountains. Big *hungry* cats. . . .

But it wasn't a cougar that pulled him out of the fork of a tree where he had decided to try to sleep.

Even as he felt the strong hand lock on to his belt and yank him down, his nostrils twitched at the unmistakable smell of an Indian.

CHAPTER 9

ARMED AND DANGEROUS

Starlight winked off cold steel as it plunged towards his chest. He was unable to twist aside but the blade struck the rocks he had in his pocket, deflecting the knife. A spark flashed as the metal grated across a piece of quartz and the Indian grunted, stepping back, startled.

Caine ducked his head, straining against the raw strength of Paco. He kicked savagely at the man's shins. The Indian snorted this time and reacted instinctively, by half-doubling, reaching down for the leg that was giving him such intense pain.

Caine's knee rose and connected with the side of Paco's head. The Indian sprawled, losing his grip on the white man. Caine twisted free, started to reach for his own knife, but changed the movement and tried to stab Paco in the eyes with pronged fingers. He missed, but tore part of the man's thin eyebrow. Blood flowed into one of those dark, murderous eyes.

The Indian grunted, a mixture of anger and surprise. He slashed with the knife but Caine dropped to the ground, clubbed one fist and smashed it, side on, into Paco's kneecap. It might not have dislodged the cap from its socket but it came close and this time Paco howled like a wolf caught in a bear trap. He sagged, starting to fall. Caine spun on to his back and drove both boots into the snarling, bloody face.

Paco hurtled backwards, crashed his head into the tree trunk. His eyes crossed and he dropped his knife. Caine firmed his boots as he stood, hammered a barrage of blows into the sinewy midriff. Paco dropped to his knees, gagging. Caine twisted his fingers in the greasy hair, smashed the man's head back into the tree again.

Breathing hard, he knelt beside the unconscious Indian, felt in the pocket of the buckskin shirt but found only tobacco and papers. Well, all donations gratefully accepted.

He found the man's knife. It was much sharper and had better steel than the ancient blade MacAdam had given him. It fitted his sheath well enough, but the man was carrying nothing else that could help him. He stripped off the rope around Paco's waist, which the 'breed used for a belt, and trussed him up, ankles and wrists, the latter tied behind the now moaning man.

Leaving Paco, he took his spear and scouted around, listening, eventually hearing the stomping of a tethered horse. He found the paint Indian pony amongst some boulders, a heavy rock holding down the ends of the reins. There was a whiteman's saddle and a Winchester rifle in the boot.

Caine snatched the weapon. The woodwork was scratched and dented. The blueing on the barrel and breech had rubbed in patches, but the lever worked smoothly enough and ejected the shells easily. A full magazine of ten and one in the breech. This Indian had learned the whiteman's way well. There were two cartons of shells in one of the beaded and decorated saddle-bags, some hardtack and a few handfuls of corn, the latter likely for the pony when Paco was on the trail.

The other saddle-bag had only one thing in it, wrapped in an old, soggy newspaper: MacAdam's scalp.

Paco cried out as Caine's boot drove brutally into his side and, semi-conscious, he rolled, discovering for the first time he was bound and a prisoner. Caine held out the scalp which still had some blood dripping from the hair. Paco looked up at him with blank eyes.

'You son of a bitch! Why the hell'd you have to kill a good man like that!'

The Indian's expression didn't change. There was no fear in his dark eyes. Maybe a spark of hate, but not even much of that. Here was a man who wasn't bothered in the least by killing. He would do it with one hand while chomping on a greasy steak, or stroking his squaw with the other hand.

Caine squatted in front of him, holding the rifle. 'It's tolerably fresh. How long since you left MacAdam's?'

'Long enough to track you.'

Caine nodded slowly. 'Who's with you? Killane?'

'He come. And others.'

'How far behind?'

No reply. He wanted to smash this stoical face with the rifle butt but instinctively he knew it would not get him an answer.

'I'm going to kill you before I leave,' Caine told him, but the words brought absolutely no response. 'It'll be painful. . . .' There was a faint flick in the dark eyes but nothing more. 'You'll still be crying when the Great Spirit comes for your rotten soul. S'pose I take *your* scalp and ride out with it? Bury it deep where it can never be found? Be no Happy Hunting Grounds for you then. You gotta be complete to qualify – if that's the word. Right?'

Paco was showing signs of alarm now, writhing, but stopping when it hurt his damaged knee. He breathed hard and fast through pinched nostrils, staring at his captor.

Caine rolled a cigarette from Paco's tobacco sack and leaned against a nearby tree as he smoked. 'You got till I finish it,' he said, holding up the burning cigarette.

With the other hand he took Paco's knife from his sheath and tested the edge with his thumb.

'Not too sharp. Might have to saw quite a bit. But you go ahead and yell all you want when I start. Might bring in Killane and whoever's with him.'

'Doc Russell,' the Indian breathed, quickly, no doubt hoping a little co-operation might gain him a reprieve.

'So Campion's bought into it. Well, that didn't gain you much, feller. Anything else you'd like to tell me before I finish this smoke?'

Paco stared back; there was obvious fear stirring in his eyes now. He wasn't afraid of pain or death – but he wanted to be a whole person when he went to the Great Spirit. Otherwise *his* spirit would be left to wander between the winds for ever, with no resting place.

'Two men – Tex and Hashknife—'

'And you all worked over poor MacAdam!'

'Killane said Doc would pay in gold if we make farmer tell where you go.'

So Campion was on to the gold part already. No more time to spend here. He wanted to shoot Paco but was afraid Killane and Campion might already be close enough to hear it. He couldn't bring himself to impale the Indian on his spear, not in cold blood. In the heat of battle, sure, but not like this. And he had always hated knives for killing a man. But the sonuver had to pay for scalping MacAdam!

Cursing his weakness, Caine stood, propped the rifle against a tree, and looked around for inspiration, watched uneasily by the silent Indian.

Tex Arlin was first into the clearing, having found Paco's pinto and back-tracked from there.

He was waiting when Killane and Campion and Hashknife rode up. They all looked at the Indian slumped against the tree, blood drying in streaks and smears on his sallow face.

There was a heavy rock that must have weighed fifty pounds resting at an angle across both of the Indian's lower legs.

'Judas! He busted both his legs!' breathed Hashknife.

113

'This Caine's harder than I figured.'

'He's soft,' growled Campion. 'Or he'd've killed Paco outright.'

'Maybe he didn't want him to die outright,' said Killane. 'That's MacAdam's scalp in Paco's lap.'

Campion shrugged. 'Well, I'm not waiting around for Paco to come to. Tex, see if you can pick up Caine's trail and we'll push on.'

'What about Paco?'

'He's not going anywhere. Unless you or Hashknife want to take him back to the pen?'

'Not while you fellers go and find the gold!' Tex said coldly. 'I ain't that dumb.'

'Then do like I said; scout around for Caine's tracks.'

'Paco's rifle's missin',' Killane pointed out.

Russ Campion's mouth tightened and he nodded jerkily. 'I noticed. We'll need to ride careful. Caine was always a damn good shot when I knew him. No reason to think he's any different now.'

'Where's he headed? Any notion?'

Campion shrugged. 'Might know better when Tex picks up his tracks, but looks to me like he's going towards Dragoon County.'

'That's a helluva way from here!'

Campion nodded slowly. 'It was within ridin' distance of where we camped the night Mulvaney took the mule and six bars of gold. Wasn't called that then, of course.'

'Hell! We'll be there till Doomsday if we gotta search the whole of the county.'

'That's why we have to catch up with Caine,'

Campion told him wearily. 'Mulvaney must've told him where he hid the gold before he died. Caine wouldn't't've run otherwise.'

'No? He wasn't havin' any vacation in the Big Pen, you know. I can vouch for that.'

'Yeah, but he and Mulvaney got along pretty good. He'd've told Caine where, once he knew he was gonna croak.'

'Well, let's go find out. . . .'

And hard on the heels of his words, Tex's cry reached them from across the slope.

'Looks like his hoss run off, but he's found it again and the tracks're still headin' south-east.'

There was a rush to mount and ride away from where the unconscious Indian sat very still with his shattered legs.

And MacAdam's scalp resting bare inches from one limp hand.

Caine's tracks led them into a dry wash. Tex Arlin immediately reined down, hipping in the saddle.

'Don't like this!' he called to the others. 'Too many places on the walls a man can set up for an ambush.'

As he spoke, a rifle cracked, the echo of the shot whiplashing and slapping back and forth down the wash. Tex's mount went down in a flurry of hoofs and spilling saddle gear as the rider went flying over the horse's head.

The others scattered, seeking cover in a hurry.

The second shot kicked dust and grit beside Tex's rolling body, stinging his face. He threw himself in close against the warm quivering body of the horse, reached across tentatively for the rifle butt poking out of the saddle scabbard. He got it free and had just dropped back when a third bullet thunked into the mount's carcass.

The others had found shelter: Campion behind rocks, a deadfall for Killane, while Hashknife's choice was belly flat in a hollow in the ground.

Their rifles began firing towards the smoke drifting up from a narrow cleft. Killane worked his lever and trigger in a fast volley, placing his bullets in the wall just above head height. Mostly the lead just gouged dirt and a few stones, but two struck protruding rocks and ricocheted across to the opposite wall and back again the other way.

Caine was pinned down by that volley, knowing he was lucky not to have been hit. He hurriedly backed out of the cleft into a wider area, below which he had his mare ground-hitched. As he slid around to a new position, he noticed the mare's ears pricked and the alert eyes. He hoped it wouldn't spook and fuss enough to drag the reins out from under the rock holding them down. Now was no time to be left afoot with these three coming after him.

They must have found Paco and abandoned the man with his shattered legs. Well, that was someone else's problem; he had enough on his plate trying to get out of here alive.

He had figured he might end the pursuit here, but sun glare had thrown his aim a little; the bullet had missed Tex Arlin by a hair but found lodging in the

116

horse's tossing head.

He settled beneath a tilted boulder and felt immediately uncomfortable with a couple of tons of granite hanging only inches above him. But he pushed the thought to the back of his mind, beaded one of them down there ducking for cover in a safer position. The man – Hashknife as it happened – stopped in mid-stride and spun almost in an about-face before dropping. Caine heard the man's gun clatter as it fell. He shifted aim quickly to where sunlight ran in a silver streak along a gun barrel tracking him. He triggered and saw dust spurt into the rifleman's face, sending the man rearing back.

It wasn't Killane so it must be Russ Campion. The man looked heavier than when he had known him in the army and was dressed way better, but then a scarecrow would be better dressed than a Johnny Reb on the run during during the last days before Appomattox.

Killane almost nailed him as he stared at Campion. The bullet flicked Caine's hat brim, raising dust, clipping the edge of the felt and buzzing close to his shoulder in its passing. He crouched lower, could see beneath the tilted boulder, and watched Killane changing position, no doubt cursing his missed shot at Caine.

Caine lifted the rifle and fired instantly; he was quick of eye and had the true rifleman's gift, subconsciously driving his shot into his target. As he did this time. But he didn't kill Killane, the lead gouged across the deputy warden's left tricep, ripping up the shirt and sending blood spraying.

117

Killane dropped out of sight mighty fast and Caine sent another shot after him, smiling grimly as he saw it ricochet from the rock bare inches above Killane's body. He paused to thumb home four or five shells through the loading gate, dropped back and down a level, hearing lead raking his previous position.

Tex Arlin had found himself a better shelter and worked lever and trigger hard, raking all around the balanced boulder above Caine. But he was tucked into a tight little hollow now, safe from ricocheting bullets coming from almost any angle.

'Why you so touchy, Josh?' called Campion suddenly, sounding genuinely puzzled. 'We only want to talk.'

'That what you told MacAdam?'

'Hell, whatever happened to that sodbuster was his own fault. *We* only wanted to talk but he got froggy an' – well, never mind him. It's you I want to powwow with.'

'Not today, Russ. Not ever.'

'Aw, don't be like that. Look, there's plenty to go around. Ten bars – must be worth close to fifty thousand bucks.'

'Less the four you stole before old Mull grabbed his six.'

A brief silence. 'Yeah, must've slipped my mind. See, they never did me any good. I had to hide 'em in a hurry but it rained hard – you likely recall that night when the storm come up outta nowhere? No? Not playin' talks. OK. Fact is, I got nothing outta those bars. Rain washed away the dirt and this damn Yankee patrol come ridin' by to see what was shining in the sun after the storm had gone.'

118

There was still bitterness in Campion's voice even after all this time. It didn't surprise Caine; Russ Campion had always been like that, never forgot anything that went against what he wanted. Never forgot a hurt.

'You use that right hand of yours OK, Russ?'

After a long silence, 'Still cain't flex my fingers fully – is why I couldn't be a real doctor. I guess you'll have to pay for that sometime, Josh.'

'Wonder why that don't surprise me. Anyway, Russ, that's all I got to say. You want me to talk any more, I'll do it through Mr Winchester.'

And he blasted off six fast shots, raking the rocks where Campion lay, sending splinters thrumming from Killane's log, ricocheting lead from Tex's shelter.

Then Caine was moving – fast. He dropped off his ledge and slid a few yards, coming out only feet from where the black mare waited with suspicious eyes. It tugged violently at the rock-held reins and started to rear, but was pulled down by the reins again. Lucky that that was a heavy rock, thought Caine as he slid the hot rifle into the scabbard, pulled the reins free and leapt into the saddle.

The horse was away and at a gallop in seconds, Caine rocking wildly as he fought to get his boot into the flailing stirrup iron. He fluked it and gained control, much to the mare's chagrin, but she settled into a canter as Caine guided her around a huge boulder and cleared the wash.

He was well ahead and had disappeared into heavier timber by the time the pursuers had dragged themselves out from their cover and taken stock of their wounds.

'He's damn good with that rifle,' Killane said. He rammed a wadded kerchief through the rips in his shirtsleeve, covering the bleeding gouge in his shoulder muscle.

'Tell Hashknife in case he don't know,' Tex Arlin said tightly.

Hashknife had been hit in the lower part of his torso, the bullet ripping through muscle, bouncing off a rib and leaving it fractured. He was in pain every time he moved, but was determined to be in at the kill – Caine's kill.

Campion had mere scratches and was impatient to get on Caine's trail, unsympathetic to any of the others.

'Let's move or we'll lose him!'

'Mebbe that's not such a bad idea, losin' the bastard,' gritted Hashknife. 'He fights like a cornered grizzly and we ain't even near his gold yet.'

'We don't lose him,' snapped Campion, rubbing at the puckered scar on his right hand. 'I'll shoot the first one to drop out – and the next one to even mention it.'

He raked a murderous stare around the three wounded men.

No one said anything. When Campion moved towards his mount, the others made for their own horses.

CHAPTER 10

THREE SHOTS

Despite the prison warden trying to keep it quiet, word spread throughout Bear Creek County that there had been a successful breakout from the Big Pen.

The warden was fit to be tied, threatening murder and mayhem amongst his staff, yelling constantly for Killane. He sent men into the field to try to find his deputy but the man seemed to have disappeared, with some of the best trackers and hardcase crew, leaving the sheriff in charge.

Folk who lived in Bear Creek County were pleased at the news; they liked to see the bed-hopping warden upset and, while husbands and boyfriends were leery about trying to stop his amorous sojourns with their women, this kind of news put a smile on everyone's face.

Hell, this Frank Keller, who was supposed to have escaped, wasn't even all that dangerous. A hold-up man who fumbled a stage robbery and found himself facing the terrible Judge Cobb. Good luck, Keller – keep on runnin'! That was the general tone. Whether or not this 'Keller' could expect help from Bear Creek folk was another thing; they might not be game enough to stretch things that far. But, could be, if he was sighted, it just might not be reported. . . .

The warden was so frustrated after almost a week without resolution to the problem that he posted a reward for Keller's capture and a smaller one for information leading to his apprehension, $2,000 and $1,000 respectively.

Naturally, all this spread far and wide beyond Bear Creek County and even attracted the attention of a few bounty hunters, amateur and pros, from other states.

It also reached the ears of Ray Porteus.

Ray was still working for Jack Wall as a shotgun guard. It was an easy chore and kept a few dollars in his pockets while he waited impatiently for news from Caine.

He knew he was being mighty hopeful that Caine would make any attempt to contact him after the double-cross he had pulled. Not that Ray saw it as a double-cross; to him it was just a matter of seizing an opportunity.

Besides, the stage driver had been looking at him mighty suspiciously when he had hesitated to pick up the shotgun after Caine had been stupid enough to stumble over that rock and put himself in a vulnerable position.

But he had put on a pretty good act of a man having been scared half to death and later resenting the fact. He made it very clear to Judge Cobb how he was damn sure he was going to be Caine's first target, and thereby ensured that his pard was shipped off to Bear Creek penitentiary.

He knew Caine well enough to be sure the man would get next to Mulvaney at the first opportunity.

Now, at last, he had confirmation that his spur-of-the-moment plan was working. Why else would Caine have broken out? Ray had known how difficult it would be to do so but simply figured Caine would find a way. He was smart and, best of all, game, not afraid to take risks if he figured them necessary and likely to pay off.

As for the hardships and misery Caine would have had to endure behind the walls of the Big Pen, well, hell, they would be more than compensated for by the gold.

If he decided to share with Caine. That was something else he had to think about. But first and foremost, he had to locate Josh. It seemed that two posses of experienced men weren't having any success – and they were in the territory where Caine was likely to be.

Ray set out for that same area, knowing he had to be smarter than the posses. His two advantages were that he likely knew Caine better than any man alive and he had also known Mulvaney. Though, he grudgingly admitted, ten years in that prison would probably have changed the old soldier. Red Stevens had told them Mulvaney's heart was failing, so it was possible he had died or been close to it when Caine lit out.

And Caine wouldn't have done that unless he had learned where the gold bars were stashed.

Or would he? You could never tell with Joshua Caine. He was a man with strange principles – strange to Ray's way of looking at life, that was. If he had simply seen a chance to get out, well, he might have grabbed it and taken off. *Damnit!*

He wished he hadn't thought of that, but Ray was realistic, he looked at things from every possible angle. And the only way to find out for sure what was happening was to locate Caine.

He quit the stageline job far from Jack Wall's head office, didn't even let the man know he was leaving. The stage ran into Flintrock for turn-around and night stopover, and during that time Ray simply rode on out. He had brought his mount in, tied to the boot of the coach, three runs earlier and stashed it in the livery corrals, striking an acceptable daily rate with the liveryman.

With spare ammunition, a full grubsack and a new saddle canteen, he had walked away from the depot after collecting his pay; then he'd settled with the stables and ridden out.

Flintrock was on the extreme northern county line, right next door to Bear Creek County. He was in what he thought of as hunting territory by sun-up.

Now, all he had to do was get a line on where the posses were working, find a good Ordnance Survey map and figure out what Caine would do.

Yeah – that was all!

*

Hashknife had dropped way behind again and Campion had had enough.

'You stay put, or head on back to the posse still down there near the Big Pen. You're only slowing us down.'

Hashknife had lost a good deal of blood from his wounds, especially the one in his lower ribs, and was weak and sick. He didn't care for Campion's orders and even tried to reach for his six-gun, but his hand dropped away and he lay back against his sun-heated boulder, breathing hard, the world spinning about him.

'I – want my – share,' he grated.

'You ain't earning it,' Killane told him, agreeing with Campion that the hardcase should be left behind.

'Only – luck you – ain't hit – worse.'

'Well, guess my luck's better'n yours. How about a quick bullet now? Save you a heap of suffering?'

'No!' Hashknife found enough breath to shout that back and Killane smiled crookedly, hand on gun butt.

He looked at Campion who shook his head. 'No gunfire. It could warn Caine we're getting close. God knows where he is but I ain't taking any chances. Let's go.'

As he said this he glanced at Tex Arlin, perhaps expecting some objection, but the lanky Texan just started his mount moving forward.

So much for saddlemates and loyalty. . . .

Hashknife lay there, holding the blood-soaked rag against his body wound. If only he could work his Colt! But he wouldn't get them all before one of them finished him.

Damn! He deserved better treatment than this! He

had a deal of living to do yet before he saddled up for the Last Round-up, he thought, as he reluctantly watched the trio disappear into the dust cloud their horses raised.

Hashknife lay there, feeling his pain and growing weakness. *There must be something he could do!* He couldn't just lie here and let them get away with not only robbing him of his due, but giving him a death sentence, too.

Yeah! There *was* something. There was a chance that it could backfire and get him killed anyway, but he had to try. *Had* to. . . .

He gave them time to get deeper into the hills, then fumbled out his six-gun. It took a mighty effort and was harder than he would ever have expected, but he managed to fire three more or less evenly spaced shots, a long interval between each one as he cocked the hammer with blood-slippery hands.

He smiled, a little blood in his mouth staining his teeth, and let the smoking gun drop down at his side. Maybe those shots would alert Caine if he was close enough. That would upset their damn plans; he knew Campion was only using his wounds as an excuse to cut him out of a share in the gold – if they ever found it. He was too weak to fight back any other way. All he hoped was that Campion didn't send Tex back to finish him off, but maybe Tex wouldn't do it. They'd ridden a lot of trails together. But then, Tex had just ridden out with the others, not even looking back at his old pard. It was too late now, anyway.

With blood-sticky fingers, he reloaded the six-gun,

and waited. But he felt himself slipping away, tried to hold on to consciousness, but suddenly everything was black and he was falling, tumbling out of control.

Ray Porteus heard the three shots: the universal signal for someone in trouble or in need of help.

He wasn't a very Good Samaritan as such, but having sided Josh Caine for so long, a little, a *very* little, of the man's decency had rubbed off and he hauled rein on a high ledge, listening to the fading, cracking echoes.

Ray had been riding hard for two days. He was into the third now, and he was deep in Bear Creek County, must be approaching the general search area. But he didn't know just where he was and maybe whoever had triggered those shots might be able to tell him. Wouldn't cost much to find out; there was even the possibility it was Caine himself, signalling.

He knew better than to put much hope in *that* but he figured out the direction the shots had come from and, just before noon, he saw the wounded man slumped against a boulder. He was wearing a blood-soggy shirt, and a hat was tilted over his face.

Gun in hand, Ray walked the mount in warily, circuiting once, then climbing down. He used his rifle barrel to push the hat off, and hunkered down as Hashknife opened his droopy eyes a slit.

'Hashknife O'Hare, ain't it?' Ray said. 'Seen you gut a man in Deadwood once. You're mighty handy with a blade, but you didn't get close enough to your man this time, looks like.'

'Dun . . . dunno you.'

'No. Don't matter. What does, is I heard you worked for that loco warden at the Big Pen. Troubleshooter with that other snake, Tex Arline.' Ray smiled thinly. 'That right?'

'Go . . . hell!'

'Bound that way, I guess. But I'm here now.' Ray reached out and suddenly Hashknife screamed and was gasping for breath as Ray wiped blood off his fingers on the man's mostly unsoiled neckerchief. 'Got a touchy spot down there, huh? Well, I could give you a little doctorin' – or a lot of pain – unless you tell me what I want to know.'

Hashknife's eyes were wide now, his fear obvious. 'Why you . . . wanna do . . . that?'

'Don't wanna waste the time. But I'm willin' to spend an hour or so. Till you tell me about Josh Caine – or Frank Keller as you'd know him. You wanna be friendly and help me out?'

His fingers prodded again and Hashknife screamed. He didn't have enough breath to reply but nodded his head vigorously: *ask away*. . . .

Caine had heard the three shots, too. But they were barely audible, they were so far distant. If he hadn't been on top of a rise and sitting quietly while the mare rested in shade after the steep climb, he wouldn't have picked up the sounds.

A mite ragged, he thought, well-spaced, like someone hurt, shooting slow, having a little trouble cocking the hammer after each shot, maybe.

He could be signalling, of course, not asking for – or

expecting – help. But the thing was, someone was behind him and it was a good bet it had to be Campion's bunch. Wasn't likely any of them who fired the trio of shots. Unless . . . not unless they'd left one of the wounded behind.

He mounted the mare and fought it a little to get it going again, not down the steep slope on the far side, but just below the crest, riding west. It was dangerous, for the ground was soft and tended to slide away under the mare's hoofs. This made it protest, but also concentrate so that it didn't fall. And, best of all, the sliding earth disguised the hoofmarks. When he came to some brush he swung the mare down, but not straight down; it was too steep. He angled across the face of the slope. The mare might not be ecstatic about it, but it was better than the awkward course just below the crest.

These hills were well-clad with timber and he rode lower down the mountain until he could move into the cover of the trees. Here he took out MacAdam's map and figured this must be the Crookback Range, the south-west boundary of Dragoon County.

He grunted in satisfaction. He was heading in the right direction and, if Campion and his men didn't find his trail too soon, he would be in the Dragoon Hills by tomorrow.

Then all he had to do was search about twenty square miles of strange, rugged country, and hope to locate Mulvaney's hiding-place for the gold – without having any idea of where it was stashed.

Nothing to it, he thought grimly.

CHAPTER 11

'SEE THE DRAGON!'

Ray Porteus got more information than he had expected from the dying Hashknife.

Not only had the man been hard on Caine's trail, he had been with Campion at the interrogation of some sodbuster named MacAdam who had helped Caine, outfitted him, given him a map that might be helpful in his search.

The farmer had mentioned Dragoon County, Hash told him, and Ray had smiled.

'H-huh?' Hashknife said, barely conscious, wondering why Ray looked so pleased.

'It's OK, Hash. Just that I happen to know the old Dragon County fairly well. Been a long time since I was in there but—'

He paused. Hashknife was slowly shaking his head. 'N-not Dr-Dragon. Dra-goon. . . .'

'Ah, everyone lives there calls it Dragon County.

Clerk misspelled it one time on some legal papers and the name stuck – Also there's a. . . .'

Ray stopped. Hashknife was gasping, chest heaving in fast, shallow efforts. Strangled sounds came from the back of his throat and when he opened his mouth, blood spilled down his chin. Ray snatched his hand back from where it rested near the man's lower wound.

Hashknife O'Hare took quite a few minutes to die but by that time, Ray Porteus was mounted and riding away. He took O'Hare's six-gun and rifle with him.

The wildlife would take care of Hashknife's body. Ray had no use for him any longer and didn't aim to spend time and effort burying him.

He had a lot of hard riding to do, to catch up with Caine before Campion and his men did.

'Why you think Hash fired them shots?' asked Tex Arlin, half-hipped in the saddle, looking past Campion and Killane, back in the direction they had left O'Hare.

'Don't matter why,' Campion told him. 'He done it and Caine could've heard. No sense wastin' time going back – no point to it. We push on faster. And make sure you don't miss any of Caine's sign.'

Arlin nodded and rode a little way ahead.

'Think he's havin' second thoughts about riding out on Hash,' opined Killane. 'They'd been together a long time.'

'He can have all the thoughts he likes, long as he keeps trailin' Caine.'

Killane studied Campion. He had never thought much of the man as a sawbones when he had visited the jail and given ailing prisoners no more than basic treatment, no matter what their symptoms. But this was a harder, more cold-blooded Campion. Even his name was different. No longer Doc Russell. He had waited all these years to get a line on that gold he knew old Mulvaney had stolen, and now nothing was going to stop him getting his hands on it.

What worried Killane, who was no cream-puff, was just what was Campion going to do when he did locate the gold bars? He didn't think in terms of 'if' any longer – not now that he could see the true Russ Campion.

He was pretty sure he and Arlin wouldn't see their share as Campion had promised. *Talk's cheap.*

After they'd left Hashknife, Campion had said to the solemn Arlin, 'Three into six goes two, Tex. Two bars apiece now. Think about that, it'll brighten your day.'

But earlier, Campion had said he would take three bars as leader. To Killane, it meant Campion had no intention of sharing *any* of the gold. It was just talk.

Reaching down his outer right leg, Killane scratched as if at an itch, but then he straightened slowly, with a faint satisfied smirk just touching the corner of his mouth.

The hideaway gun was still in its built-in holster. He had had the half-boots made specially, incorporating that holster, a long time ago; as deputy warden of Big Pen he had made plenty of enemies – and not all of them were amongst the prisoners.

Now, that precaution just might pay off if Campion did try a double-cross. If so. . . .

One of them would get lead instead of gold.

According to MacAdam's map, Caine was now in the Dragoon Mountains.

He had picked out a couple of landmarks, aware that his heart was beating a little faster. The search to uncover the gold was still ahead of him but he was getting closer and he couldn't help the optimistic feeling that rose within him.

Finding Mulvaney's family, or daughter, more likely, as his wife might not still be living, would be another difficulty, and it would be mighty easy to just give up after a token search and keep all the gold. *Tempting!* But he had given Mull his word, and he would stick by it.

He would not put a limit on the search for Bertha and Eve Mulvaney. And, once he had the gold, the extra money might even make the quest easier. He could afford professional assistance.

'First, find the goddamn gold, you fool!' he chided himself aloud as he rode between two hills, feeling the chill as the mare took him into deep shadow. He glanced up at the colouring sky.

Nearing sundown. He was low on water but decided to wait until tomorrow to try to find a well or stream. Within a rough circle of boulders he made his camp, without a fire. He had only hardtack and not enough water to brew coffee. And it would be safer if there was no glow to guide in any of his pursuers.

After eating mechanically, ignoring the growling protest of a stomach that seemed forever no more than only partially satisfied, he took out Mulvaney's tin. He

133

wanted to look at that charcoal map again but he would need to light a match to do so. He was already forgoing his after-meal cigarette and there would be little point in firing up a vesta now. He folded the paper back into the old tin and placed it once more in his shirt pocket.

It could wait until daylight.

He checked the mare's hobbles and his rifle, then turned in.

The sky was streaked with rays of the rising sun when he awoke and ate another cold meal, checking his grubsack and finding he had little food left. He would have to set some snares for birds or ground squirrels or possums; hunting bigger game that required a bullet to stop it would be stupid.

He spread the paper, trying not to smear the charcoal any more, hunting a beam of direct sunlight by which to see it properly. With this extra natural brilliance he was surprised to find that he could now make out some words that had shown only as blurred smears in the dull light of an oil lamp.

He tightened his grip on the paper's edges, feeling the tension of excitement. He could now read the names on a few landmarks, even make out the crude map lines more clearly.

Looking around, he could actually recognize some features. That balanced rock that had looked like a blob earlier. It was up the draw right behind his camp; he had seen it only an hour ago when he had walked up there to relieve his bladder. Other 'blobs' turned out to be a dotted line, showing the trail he should take, passing beneath that balanced rock.

Beyond was a series of undulations and strokes which he took to indicate clefts or washaways, on a rise or a slope. These marks showed a vaguely familiar shape from some angles and if he got the focus just right. But he could never hold the image long enough to identify it.

He hadn't managed to decipher much more before he stiffened: there was a sharp, cracking sound, a small hollow *clunk*, like a horse's hoof knocking two stones together.

But he told himself it was only rocks being warmed by the sun after the chill of night. Just the same, he reached for his rifle beside him. There was already a shell in the breech and he cocked the hammer slowly, using his other hand to cram the paper back into the tin and work the lid on.

Caine stood slowly, putting the tin back into his pocket, then moved deeper into the rocks, eyes and ears straining. From here he could see the mare. Her ears were flicking. Then he stood straight up and her head turned towards the entrance to the circle of boulders.

There was a faint whickering beyond the line of rocks and Caine dropped instantly, every sense alert.

One of them must be riding a stallion: Killane, he thought, remembering the gunfight earlier, and it had likely smelled the mare with the scent of the wilds still on her.

He bet the rider, whoever he was, was cussing a blue streak because his mount had whickered, but it was too late now. Caine had been alerted and was ready to stand and fight.

Hand on the fore-end of the rifle steadied against the rock, Caine drew a careful bead on the gap where the rider would appear.

He heard the horse coming slowly and his finger tightened on the trigger, taking up the slack. The horse's shadow appeared, thrown by the early light against a grey boulder. He lifted the rifle's barrel slightly, so he would be beading the rider. . . .

But they had out-smarted him: there was no rider. They had sent the mount in when it had smelled the mare, knowing Caine would have heard and would be lying in wait.

He released the pressure on the trigger just in time. But he knew he might already have given away his posiiton if the Winchester's barrel had been visible beyond the rock where he was hidden.

A volley of whining, rockdust-spurting bullets confirmed this as he reared back, face stinging, vision blurred.

The line of lead followed him, along the natural line of his movement deduced by the shooter, rather than being aimed at a direct sighting of him. The man had judged that Caine would dodge to the right. The lead almost got him and he felt hot blood trickling down his neck from one ear. It must be cut from rock chips: there was no all-encompassing numbness as when a bullet clipped flesh.

Down on his knees now, he crawled away under the rocks, having no other choice except to charge out and hope there was only one of them. Moments later he was glad he hadn't made that wild charge.

Two more guns opened up from above, shooting into his cover diagonally and he knew they had had him spotted, probably from the first glow of daylight. *Damn fool!* He had been over-confident that he could find his way in here and take his time about settling in to a good defending position. Instead they had closed the gap during the night and someone who knew this area well had got his men in position.

There were at least three. There had been four last time they had exchanged greetings in lead, but he thought that the one called Hash had been hit pretty bad.

He would settle for three until he had proof otherwise. They seemed to have a lot of ammunition, judging by the number of shots that raked his cover. Rolling on to his back, clutching the Indian's old Winchester close to his chest, he used heels and shoulders to work his way beneath the boulders. One scraped the rifle and momentarily jammed his fingers against the metal work of the breech. He had a sensation of being crushed and had to hold back from instinctively heaving harder and faster. This was a move he had to make inch by inch – and he would be lucky if some of the ricocheting lead hadn't found him before he got free of this cramped space.

Then his head and the crushed-in hat protruded into sudden space and he could turn to see where he was. Sun burned across his eyes in a searing flash and there was redness and shooting yellow streaks behind his snap-closed eyelids. He partly opened them and glimpsed a patch of blue sky while still working his body forward.

In a moment he was free of the crushing weight of the boulders, coarse sand having worked down his collar, scraping his upper shoulders and back. Panting, he was glad to see that the bullets weren't penetrating into this part of the rocks. He got to his knees and was hauling himself upright when a thin stream of gravel trickled down on to his clutching hand.

His knuckles were white. He snapped his head up, glimpsed a man's boots, and the scuffed and dirty cuffs of the trousers. Above this was a rifle barrel, probing, swinging towards his face.

Caine dropped on to his back, the rifle coming across his chest and rising vertically. His single shot lifted the man above him clear off the rock. There was a gurgling grunt and the boots did a brief, frantic dance, missed footing, then the body crashed down. Caine rolled aside just in time and when he looked he saw it was Tex Arlin. The bullet had gone in under the arch of his ribs and travelled upwards, through the major organs of heart and lungs, exited just under Tex's jaw and then gone on to lift the top of his head off.

Caine had seen much prettier sights but, while the other two guns were still firing into the other area of the rocks, he took off Arlin's gun belt and buckled it swiftly about his own waist. It seemed strange after all this time, having the weight of cartridges and a Colt dragging at his hips.

'He's got Tex!' Killane shouted.

Campion was too smart to answer and give away his position, but Caine heard boots scraping hurriedly over rocks and figured one or both of them were making their way to a position where they could see into this section.

Tex Arlin's rifle had fallen from his grip as he died but it must have slipped down between the boulders for Caine couldn't see it. He was still stuck with Paco's old weapon, but why should he complain? So far it had served him well enough.

Another shadow appeared, this time of a man clambering over rocks, six-gun in one hand, rifle held awkwardly in the other. The man paused suddenly, poised ready to leap down into the area where Caine stood. His face was square-jawed and suddenly greyish-yellow when he saw Caine. It was Killane and he had been caught flat-footed.

But he was a fast thinker: instead of following through and jumping down, he threw himself backwards as Caine fired. The lead cleaved air, ricocheted from a high boulder far behind Killane. The deputy warden had landed between rocks, on his back on a patch of sand.

Caine ran forward, levering a fresh shell into the breech, seeing his quarry through a gap in the rocks where one was stacked on top of two more at the lower level. Killane must have seen him through the same gap from his side, and there was a moment of panic that registered on his trail-grimed face, before he spun on to his belly, dug in his elbows and brought up his Colt, blazing.

The bullet almost made it through the gap in the boulders, but clipped one side and tumbled, shrieking away in wild ricochet. Caine, still running forward on a straight line with the gap, fired the rifle from the hip, levering twice.

Killane's body jumped as a slug caught him in the chest and dumped him down on one side, huddled at the base of a boulder.

Then Caine was punched forward as if kicked by a mule, his left shoulder numbed. His rifle struck a rock and jarred from his hand as he crashed into another rock and spilled awkwardly, going down to one knee. Grinning, Campion appeared above him on a slab of sandstone, smoking Colt angled down.

'Well, this looks like it, Josh. Where's all that sass you used to have, you and Ray Porteus? Huh? Many's the time I wanted to give both of you the back of my hand right across your mouths, but Mulvaney stopped it. Why he liked you, I dunno but. . . . Uh-uh! Don't you try for that gun!'

Caine eased back, shoulder hurting now, blood spreading on his shirt and running down his arm.

'Better not kill me, Russ. You dunno where Mull stashed that gold.'

'Wonder if you do? Eh? We'll find out. Now you just stay put and I'll come and ask you a couple of questions. I'll be close enough to look right into your eyes so I'll know if you're lyin'. . . .'

He started down, stepping surely from rock to rock. But one rolled a couple of inches under his weight and his arms flailed wildly.

Caine's newly acquired Colt appeared in his right hand, firing twice, very fast shots, one right on top of the other. Campion spun with the strike of the lead, stared in shock, still trying to lift his own pistol. Caine was about to shoot again, but saw the sudden white as the man's eyes rolled up, and Russ Campion crashed down between the rocks. His neck twisted at a very odd angle, making a crunching sound as it did so.

There was a sudden crack behind him. He staggered as something fanned his cheek. He spun, and saw Killane sprawled on his back, a derringer in his right hand, fighting to hold on long enough to put the second ball into Caine.

Then a rifle blasted from above Caine's head, and Killane was smashed back by a bullet taking him through the head.

Dazed, Caine squinted as he looked up and saw a slim shape in blurred silhouette against the morning sky.

'One you owe me, Josh,' Ray Porteus called down, waving his free hand.

'Might partly make up for that double-cross you pulled.' Caine was surprised at how breathless he was.

'Aw, it worked out OK. You'll soon see. Can you make it up here? Got somethin' to show you.'

Caine was hurting but holstered the Colt and wadded a kerchief over his shoulder wound. He started to clamber up, then had to stop and get his breath. He glanced up.

Ray was sitting now, holding the rifle easily, casually pointed in Caine's direction. 'Gonna take all day?'

'Better be – worth – seein'.'

Ray laughed, came lower and extended his right hand. Caine took it and was half-hauled up on to Ray's higher rock.

'Well?'

'There. . . .' Ray pointed to the next range across, almost bare of trees, but with many grey boulders and a few stunted bushes.

'What?' Caine's voice bore an edge of irritation. 'One more mountain to cross? That what you're showing me?'

Ray scowled. 'Open your eyes! Look at it! Look at all them shadows. See a pattern there? Best time of day to catch it right now.'

Caine frowned. 'Well, if I stretch it some, I s'pose it looks a bit like a . . . lizard, sort of crouching—'

'Not a lizard, you dumb bastard! A *dragon*! Can't you see the dragon?'

CHAPTER 12

DRAGON FIRE

'How did you know about the dragon?'

'Hell, I spent a lot of time around here. After the Old Man cleared off with the neighbour's wife, her husband moved in with Ma. Not a bad feller. Mustanger. Took me all over with him, chasin' broncs. We spent a deal of time in this here area, camped out and so on. Even after Ma died he took care of me for a spell till someone backshot him. . . .' Ray's voice drifted off and his eyes took on a faraway look. 'Found the skunk a couple years later.' He flicked his gaze to Caine. 'He burned to death in his cabin. Caught fire and somethin' blocked the door so he couldn't get out. Just before I joined the army, it was.'

That was the first time Ray had admitted anything like that, even in a roundabout way. Somehow it didn't surprise Caine as much as he thought it ought to.

'Yeah, but the dragon, that hill yonder. . . ?'

Ray smiled crookedly. 'You might recollect, Mull an' me got that long chore, takin' Yankee prisoners down through Missouri? You was away collectin' your medal or somethin'. I guess Mull was kinda lonely, and he talked a lot. I only half-listened. He said he worked for a mining company once and their engineers tested out this dragon hill. Seems the whole area was once a swamp and there was a lot of rotting roots and reeds and stuff. They reckoned it was too dangerous for men to work in: a gas was given off by that rubbish and could be poisonous, so they gave up on the idea of minin' it. Even then Mull was callin' the Dragoons the Dragons and he told me he and a pard was chased by a bunch of Yankees one time and they hid in caves in the Dragon. Spent three whole days in there, sick with breathin' that lousy gas, the Yankees searchin', mighty keen to get 'em – but they eventually gave up, all coughin' and splutterin'. Mull never said what happened to his pard but he got out OK, had some lung trouble later on that laid him low. He said the constant coughing strained his heart and that was the start of his real problems with his health. Slowed him down a good deal from what I gather. He must've remembered that hill when he and Red Stevens and Campion were passin' through to the north of here with the gold bars. It's not all that far off. I guess he decided to take his share, stashed it away down here.'

Ray paused, smiling crookedly. 'Old sonuver had a hunch they weren't gonna make it to the border with the gold so he was makin' sure he had what he wanted first. Can just imagine how Red Stevens and Campion took that piece of news!'

Caine agreed that that was how it probably was. 'So it's a good chance the gold's somewhere in those caves.'

Ray nodded, soberly. 'Sittin' there, doin' no one any good.' Suddenly he grinned. '*But. . .*! I did a lot of explorin' in that Dragon Hill as a kid. It does stink a bit but that didn't stop me. Even then I was pretendin' I was gonna find some hidden treasure, left by outlaws or somethin'. Long time back, but this is almost like a – a dream comin' true.'

'Lot of years have passed, Ray.'

'If you mean, could I still find my way about in there . . . I reckon I can.'

'We can.'

Their eyes met and Ray tensed. 'Meanin'?'

'Meaning two of us searching can do it in half the time. Once we find the gold, then we have to look for Mull's daughter. It's possible his wife's still alive, too.'

Ray built a cigarette, lit it and gave it to Caine, then rolled himself one. When it was drawing he said quietly,

'Me, I don't care whether Mull's kin are alive or not. I got no interest in 'em.'

Caine had been waiting for that. 'I have. I gave him my word I'd try to find them. Half the gold is theirs.'

Ray drew on his cigarette, exhaled and shook his head slowly, face screened a little by the smoke.

'That was *your* deal. I wasn't there.'

'No,' Caine cut in harshly. 'You weren't the one doing time in the Big Pen.'

Porteus waved it away. 'If one of us hadn't done time there and gotten next to Mulvaney, we wouldn't know where to look. Just the luck of the draw it was you.'

'No, Ray. I don't figure it was luck in any shape or form. I wouldn't've pulled what you did over the stage hold-up. Not to a man who was s'posed to be my pardner.'

'Know damn well you wouldn't. But I seen right off it was a chance to get close to that twenty thousand dollars. Hell, you weren't in the pen long. You'll make damn good money, Josh!'

'Don't matter how much or how little I make. I gave my word to Mull.'

Ray smoked on in silence and eventually crushed out his cigarette. His face was bleak when he looked at Caine and met the man's cold stare.

'Any gold given away comes outta your share. And if it's *half,* and that's what you promised Mull you'd give his daughter. . . .' He paused, shrugged, smiling crookedly. 'You ain't gonna come out of it too damn rich, Josh.'

'Mebbe you'll grubstake me.'

'And mebbe I won't.' Ray's eyes glittered now. There was no trace of banter in his words. Here he was, laying it on the line, and ready to take on Caine's resistance if he had to.

'Then I'll have to go back to riding the grubline. I've been there before.'

'We both have. Too damn often and for too damn long, you always griped. You won't want to go back to it.'

'I don't have any choice, I'll manage.'

Ray stood now, restlessly pacing a few steps one way,

then coming back. He stopped in front of where Caine sat on a deadfall, his left arm tucked in the front of a shirt Ray had given him from his saddle-bags. Supporting the arm in that way took a lot of the strain off the wounded tricep, but there was still plenty of pain and Caine wanted this ended, one way or another, pronto.

'Ray, I've told you how it is.'

'Josh, I've told you how it's gonna be.'

They tried to stare each other down. At last Caine rose slowly to his feet, swaying a little but trying to cover it. Ray tensed, right hand inching towards the butt of his Colt.

'What you gonna do?' he asked quickly, jumping back a step.

'We're gonna get this settled. Right here. Right now.'

Ray licked his lips, then reminded Caine, 'I saved your neck just a little while ago.'

'And I'm obliged. Told you I was willing to let it square away for getting me put in the Big Pen. Which would bring us back on the old footing.'

'Share and share, you mean?'

'That's how it's always been. We find the bars, you take your three. I'll take the others, and see if I can find Eve Mulvaney.'

'Hell, she's likely married with a slew of kids! You won't even know her married name.'

'If she can be found, I'll do it.'

'Take you the rest of your damn life.'

'Might give up before then, but I aim to make a damn good try. You'll have your half, Ray. What's your beef?'

Ray chewed at his bottom lip, frowning. 'That ain't what sticks in my craw. I know you'll stick to the sharin'.' Porteus hesitated. 'But it galls me that someone we don't even know is gonna get as much as I am, without havin' to do one damn thing for it.'

'She's Mull's daughter, Ray, and he stashed the gold in the first place.'

'It's Rebel gold! We all fought and bled for it. She's done nothin' to earn it!'

Quietly, Caine said, 'It's *my* share I'm giving her, Ray. You've got no say in it.'

Porteus made a surly gesture. 'It – don't set right with me, that's all.'

'It sets right with me. I can do what I like with my share – which, by the way, I don't have. Nor do you have yours. Which means this argument is kind of stupid.'

Ray's frown deepened and then he nodded. 'Right! Let's go find it first, then we can sort out what happens to it and who gets what.'

'That's already settled.'

Porteus glared, then nodded jerkily. 'Let's go, dammit!'

They made torches from bundles of dry branches broken from some of the brush growing on the hillside. It would be the dragon's left flank, if it was related to the hill's resemblance to the mythical creature.

Caine had to admit it: get the light just right and the way the shadows fell on the boulders did make it look like a crouching dragon: one egg-shaped boulder was the eye, a cutbank made a mouth in perfect relation to the jutting rocks above for the head. Even the lone patch of brush looked like one of the undersized wings these imaginary monsters were supposed to have. The back and tail, with serrations – broken parts of the ridge outlined against the sky – finished the impression, best seen in early-morning light.

With the sun directly overhead at noon, it was just a rock-studded, mostly bare hill, hardly large enough to call a mountain. The dragon part was all shadow and applied imagination.

Ray stood and studied the slopes for a while before scouting along the lower edges, then he started to climb up near the cutbank mouth. He waved to Caine who was moving up the slope at a slow pace. His wounds were painful and he had lost a deal of blood as well as a lot of sleep; his body had taken a hammering since he had quit that damn cell in the Big Pen, where his diet had left a lot to be desired.

Ray strolled back from examining the mouth, dusting off his clothes. 'Yeah, thought I remembered. There's a way in back there, all right. You need a hand?'

Caine shook his head and kept climbing at the same slow pace. Ray moved impatiently.

'Listen, you're takin' too damn long. I'm goin' in. If I come to a fork where the tunnel splits in two, I'll leave a torch burnin' in the side I take. OK?'

Caine waved and sat on a rock to get his breath. He was feeling a good deal weaker than he had reckoned on, but the slope was deceiving; it was a lot steeper than it looked and working around those giant boulders required quite an effort, using only his good arm. His shoulder was aching right up into his neck now, stiffening it, giving him a headache. He had his bundles of torches slung across his back with a length of rope, being careful not to let it come in contact with his wounded shoulder.

Straightening with a small grunt of effort, he watched Ray disappear into the black maw at the rear of the overhang. *A man in a hurry.*

Caine saw only trouble ahead. Ray was letting his greed take over, and if they managed to find the gold, he felt Ray would not be satisfied with just three of the bars. Probably he would be if it was just the two of them involved.

But he couldn't rest easy thinking about Mulvaney's daughter getting a half-share, equal to his own for nothing, as he saw it. He had fought in a bloody war for years, battled to make a living through Reconstruction, done time on Larsen's chain gang, endured all kinds of hardships and in his mind he had earned what he obviously thought of as his gold.

Its origins didn't bother Caine. No one could legally lay claim to that gold, as the Confederacy no longer existed. It was first come, first served, and the devil take the hindmost.

He couldn't say, flatly, that he didn't care about the gold. It would be real nice to have a nest egg like that drop in your lap. But maybe it would be too much too quickly for someone like himself who was used to working hard just to stay alive, bending the law occasionally and taking the consequences! He wasn't sure what he would do with all that gold if he was unable to find Eve Mulvaney, or whatever her name was if she was married. So he didn't even think about it.

He would feel easy enough about keeping his promise to Mulvaney. It wouldn't bother him *not* to have the gold, but it would bother him not to try his best to find her.

He unslung his bundle of torches, separated them, counting six. He slung the rope across his chest and stuck five torch bundles under it on his left side. The sixth one he lit and waved it to get it alight as evenly as possible. Then he ducked his head, though there was no need, it was just an instinctive move. He made his way into the dark maw of the dragon's mouth.

His nostrils caught the musty smell of old earth and another, almost indefinable odour. It gave him a bad taste in the back of his throat and he spat. Then he remembered, one time up in Indiana they had to retrieve ammunition hidden for them in an old mine. The props were rotted and about to give way and they worked hard and fast to load all the heavy boxes on to the waiting wagons, some men coughing so violently they threw up and were too weak to be of much use.

It was this kind of stink, he recalled. The lieutenant in charge of the ammunition party had been a college man before the war and he said it was marsh gas, or methane, to give it its proper name. He added that this area had been a swamp with monster lizards and massive flying creatures in days gone by. '*Long gone by,*' the officer had stressed with a crooked smile. 'But they've left us a legacy in this gas. Tell the men there is a complete ban on smoking and only to use lanterns, no naked flames. Just to be on the safe side. You never know with these strange gases.'

Caine felt it in the back of his throat but didn't feel the need to cough or strangle – only to spit. He called to Porteus but although he heard his own voice echoing away down the twisting passage Ray did not answer.

There was a warm air current against his face and the smell of the burning torch. He could follow that all right, and he groped his way along the tunnels. There was sign where the mining company survey team had entered, a few their temporary props still in place, one of them splintered and collapsed. But mostly the tunnel walls were a lot smoother than he had expected. Curiosity got the better of him at one stage and he stopped, holding his dying torch close to the wall. It looked like rock that had been . . . melted.

Maybe there was some volcanic history to this dragon hill as well, he decided, and these were ancient lava tunnels. *Never mind the theories: get moving*. The sooner they were out of this gloomy place the better he would feel.

He took another torch bundle from his rope sling and lit it from the other one before it died. Briefly, he had two torches blazing and they threw a wave of flickering light well ahead.

He heard a clunking sound and rounded a bend, calling Ray's name again. This time Porteus answered, though he was a good distance ahead by the sound of his voice.

'It's OK, Josh. Follow this tunnel. I've come to a fork. Won't leave a torch burnin' 'cause I think I might need 'em all, but I'm going down the left hand tunnel. The left – hand – tunnel. OK?'

'Yeah. Listen, maybe we better go easy with these torches, wait'll we can get some lanterns. I just remembered. . . .'

Ray wasn't listening. 'This stink's gettin' worse. Must be goin' deeper, too. Floor's anglin', so watch yourself. . . .'

The voice trailed away and by now Caine's first torch had gone out and he had only the light of the other. He held it out in front, shielding his eyes from sparks and burning bits that floated towards him.

Ray must be travelling fast, Caine decided, stumbling and slipping on the moist ground under foot. The musty, rotten vegetable stench was stronger and he was sure the floor slanted away under foot, so Ray was probably right when he said he thought the tunnel was descending.

He reached the fork, where a barrier of black and glistening rock divided the path, a narrow tunnel branching to the left, a bigger one to the right.

How did Ray choose? What made him decide to take the smaller, left-hand tunnel. . . ?

There was no use calling out. Caine ducked his head and turned into the low-roofed tunnel, holding the torch high. It scraped the roof several times and he knew it was getting smaller, more cramped.

He found himself breathing harder and faster and consciously tried to make it more regular and normal. He wasn't usually claustrophic, but he hated monstrous weights above him, just as he had when squirming

153

under those precariously balanced boulders back at the circle where he had shot it out with Campion and the others.

But he had a whole damn mountain almost sitting on his shoulders here! A million tons, probably more, ten million. . . .

He stopped, both his body and his thoughts. He was crouched way down now and his shoulder had hit the walls a few times. It was not only narrowing from above, it was reducing rapidly in its complete diameter. Breathing *was* getting harder! He wasn't imagining it.

'*Ray! Ray! You there. . . ?*'

Only his own voice threw the words back in his sweating face.

This tunnel was angling down to God knew where – maybe all the way to hell.

He couldn't see any glow.

Maybe the tunnel turned sharply and expanded beyond the bend. He stumbled, tried to stand too tall and cracked his head on the stony roof. That awful, bitter, foul taste in the back of his throat was making him feel nauseous. . . .

Or something was.

He turned and started back the way he had come, definitely having to climb now.

Why the hell would Ray come down here. . . ?

The answer was simple: he *didn't*! Ray had sent him down – but why? Had he spotted the gold and wanted Caine to become lost in the labyrinth so he could keep it all? Had he tried to divert him into some pocket of concentrated gas?

Why didn't matter: Ray had tipped his hand. He was going to try and lose Caine in here, leave him to rot, or at least be trapped long enough for him to get the gold out.

'Damn you, Josh! I knew you'd figure it out!'

He glimpsed Ray just as his second torch bundle burned low. He rubbed it viciously along the wall, breaking off the glowing twigs and scattering them, leaving him in darkness.

There was a glow up ahead somewhere, coming from around a bend, it looked like. Colt in hand now, he groped his way forward.

A six-gun roared deafeningly and he heard a bullet screech along the wall. He dropped flat, held his fire. Ray triggered again, three fast shots this time, the roar ramming against Caine's ears as if he was in the centre of a thunderstorm.

Ray must be just putting his hand around the corner of the rock divider and shooting into the smaller tunnel – there would be little chance of missing his target in such a confined space.

But he did.

The lead whined off the smooth rock of the wall, ricocheting from one side to the other, zigzagging down into the dark depths where Caine had turned back. He was flat on his belly and knew if he fired, Ray would simply angle down his gun's barrel and shoot so that the bullet travelled a few inches above the sloping floor.

And it would find him, for sure.

What he had to do was get the hell out of here – and

155

the only way out was in the direction of that blazing gun.

Ray shot twice more. Caine figured his gun was empty now and he would be reloading. *No time to hold a mental debate. Run like hell.*

He did.

Crouching, wound hurting, jettisoning the remaining unused torch bundles, he started running uphill, crouching, finding it hard to breathe, maybe because of the gas, maybe the way he was bent double and his legs pounded up almost into his chest with each step. He wasn't game to straighten up any in case the roof was still low; he would scalp himself or worse if he hit the rock-studded tunnel roof running like this.

There were no more shots from Ray Porteus and then he reached the main tunnel where he had come in.

He glimpsed Ray crouched against the wall, on one knee, thumbing cartridges home into his Colt's cylinder, dropping one in his hurry to close the loading gate when he saw Caine. He fired wildy.

Josh twisted, still running and fired twice. Ray shuddered, was slammed back against the wall, falling forward, putting one hand down for support – the hand with his gun in it. His head was hanging, blood dribbling from his half-open mouth.

Caine paused, cocked pistol covering Porteus as the man lifted his head slowly.

'You . . . think you . . . won? Uh-uh.' he stammered. 'No gold . . . only splintered boxes . . . someone's found . . . it.'

'Then why did you try to lose me in that side tunnel, then?'

'Didn't know the . . . gold was . . . gone at the time. Knew you'd figured . . . I . . . I sent you into that dead end an' would try to . . . nail me for it. But there's a . . . a pool of . . . liquid gas where I went. Ground's sodden with . . . it. I dropped my torch and the . . . ground . . . started burnin'. It'll reach the . . . pool and . . . blow up. Get outta here. . . .'

Caine holstered his gun, lunged forward and grabbed Ray. He backed up as fast as he dared, seeing the entrance of the dragon's mouth a long way off. Ray was making unintelligible sounds and then Caine felt the ground tremble beneath his feet. Everything seemed to sway, close in and then recede, trembling again – dirt and rocks falling.

There was a rumble – increasing – roaring like a locomotive hurtling through the tunnel. He saw the wall of flames back there where Ray had come from, growing, flaring, concentrating into a fireball, squeezed into an almost solid column of fire by the narrow tunnel. . . .

'Christ! *Go!*' Ray roared the word, probably with the last breath in his lungs. Caine tightened his grip, lunged for the entrance and threw himself and his burden to the left, over the edge, away from the cutbank.

He felt the heat sear him, smelled his own hair as it was singed, and rolled down the slope. He came to a halt against a rock and, dazed, looked up in time to see the gout of red flame spew out of the tunnel mouth with a roar and a fiery tongue almost a hundred yards long.

There was a great muffled drumming and the earth swayed. Dust and falling rocks collapsed the cutbank and the overhang came down in a massive cloud of dust, sealing the tunnel and any fires burning in the bowels of the Dragon.

There wasn't a lot left of Ray Porteus to bury after the bouncing rocks had crushed his body, but Caine managed it somehow. He even made a crude cross by tying together a couple of more or less straight twigs.

As he pushed it into the newly turned soil he wondered whether Ray had sent him into that small downsloping tunnel so that the fire would be sure to devour him. Or did he think that the fire would roar along the main tunnel, straight past the entrance to the smaller one and leave Caine safe?

He would never know, but he knew which version he preferred to believe. *Stupid! Fooling yourself!*

Maybe. But they had been through a lot together, Caine and Ray. The good times had outnumbered the bad.

His hands were trembling so much that he couldn't make a cigarette and he decided to leave it until his nerves had settled down. He pressed back against a boulder, above a small draw where his mare and Ray's horse cropped some grass in companionship.

No gold. But maybe he would still look for Eve Mulvaney.

It might be some sort of comfort to her to know her

father had tried to make amends for the ill-treatment of herself and her mother.

And if she was married and had a family of her own, it would be something good to tell her children: that their grandfather had been a decent man, flawed, but basically decent. . . .

Just like a lot of other men.

Perhaps most men.